TROUBLE IN BUGLAND

William Kotzwinkle

TROUBLE
IN BUGLAND

A COLLECTION OF
INSPECTOR MANTIS MYSTERIES

PROFUSELY ILLUSTRATED BY
Joe Servello

DAVID R. GODINE, PUBLISHER
Boston

First published in 1983 by
David R. Godine, Publisher, Inc.
Post Office Box 450
Jaffrey, New Hampshire 03452

Library of Congress Cataloging in Publication Data
Kotzwinkle, William.   Trouble in Bugland.
Summary: A quick-witted insect sleuth, patterned after Sherlock Holmes,
displays his brilliant powers of deduction in solving five mysteries.
[1. Insects—Fiction. 2. Mystery and detective
stories] I. Servello, Joe, ill. II. Title.
PZ7.K855TR 1983   [Fic]   83-49338
ISBN 1-56792-070-5

Third softcover printing, 2015
Printed in China

Trouble in Bugland was set by Maryland Linotype Composition Co.
in linotype Caledonia, a typeface designed by the great American calligrapher
and graphic artist W. A. Dwiggins. This clear and classic face was inspired by
the work of Scotch typefounders, and particularly by the transitional faces
cut by William Martin for Bulmer around 1790. The display face for the
chapter openings and title page is, in fact, linotype Bulmer, also based on a
face cut by Martin and used in the famous Boydell Shakespeare of 1791.
Book design by Kathleen Westray.

CONTENTS

For J. Henri Fabre

"Oh, my pretty insects . . ."

THE CASE OF
The Missing Butterfly

THE DISAPPEARANCE of Miss Juliana Butterfly brought two familiar figures through the fog—one of them tall and slow-moving, the other short and quick.

"A most disturbing thing," said Doctor Hopper, the shorter of the two, and a regular assistant to Inspector Mantis, the lean and keen-sighted scholar of crime, who now spoke, in the swirling mist.

"Miss Juliana is a circus performer, is she not?"

"A bareback rider." Doctor Hopper tapped his cane lightly on the pave. "One of the loveliest creatures ever to circle the ring."

"I see," said Inspector Mantis, with a sidelong glance toward his friend. "And did you enjoy yesterday's performance?"

Doctor Hopper looked up with surprise. "Why, how did you know I was there?"

"That bit of straw which still clings to your trouser cuff—" He touched Hopper's scarf. "—a piece of peanut shell here. And—" Inspector Mantis gestured with his long arm. "—you have cotton candy in your mustache."

Doctor Hopper frowned, and tidied himself up. "I must say, Mantis, you amaze me, as usual. Is nothing hidden from you?"

"Much is hidden, Doctor. Much too much." And saying so, Inspector Mantis fell silent, his long arms locking behind his back as he walked, a sign that he was giving the mystery careful thought; for Miss Juliana was not the only butterfly to have disappeared of late. Dozens of the beautiful creatures had vanished, to none knew where.

The inspector's smoldering pipe went out, and the city blocks went by, one after the other, but still he said nothing, until the outskirts of the city had been reached and the sounds of a circus came from ahead. "Well, then, Doctor, since you've been here before, I suggest you lead the way."

Doctor Hopper obliged, conducting them through the circus grounds, to the main tent, where Miss Juliana had last performed. They were met there by P. T. Barnworm, the owner of the circus.

"Terrible, terrible, terrible." Barnworm wrung his many hands. "Miss Juliana was my star performer!"

"We share your feelings," said Doctor Hopper. "She was wonderful to behold."

P. T. Barnworm took a challenging step toward Mantis. "Can you find her?"

"We shall do our best." Inspector Mantis was already looking toward the center ring. He pointed toward a spot halfway around. "I see it was from precisely—*there*—that she was abducted."

P. T. Barnworm raised his eyebrow. "How did you know?"

"Much is hidden, Doctor. Much too much."

"Would you have any objections to my looking more closely?" Inspector Mantis, not waiting for an answer, stepped toward the circle of sawdust.

P. T. Barnworm turned to Doctor Hopper. "It happened in the middle of the show. The lights went out for a second. When they came back on—Miss Juliana was gone!"

"A wretched business." Doctor Hopper gazed at the ring, where just last night he'd so enjoyed the sight of Miss Juliana balancing on her trained horseflies. Now the ring was miserably empty, save for Inspector Mantis snooping around it, magnifying glass in his hand.

"What is he doing?" asked Barnworm.

"His ways are peculiar," said Doctor Hopper. "But I daresay he's already found something."

Inspector Mantis came out of his crouch and put his magnifying glass away.

"Well?" asked Barnworm, cracking his whip nervously at his side, as if Mantis were an unpredictable animal in his circus menagerie.

"We must bid you good-day now, Mr Barnworm, and trust that your show will go on as usual tonight. If you have any other butterflies in your company, I suggest you keep them under close watch."

Inspector Mantis turned toward the exit and Doctor Hopper followed him. "Well, Mantis," asked the doctor impatiently, "what did you find?"

"Miss Juliana was seized by a gang of Assassin Bugs; their traces are everywhere around the ring, and at this doorway, as well."

"A moment, Mantis," said Doctor Hopper. "I have something sticky on my shoe."

"Exactly," said Mantis, waiting until Hopper had removed his shoe; he then pointed toward the sole. "That sticky substance, which you have just stepped in, is of a most singular kind, exuded only by the Assassin Bug. You'll note the dust clinging to it—another characteristic of the Assassin—they gather dust wherever they go. In this case, it was sawdust, which allowed them to pass unnoticed into the very center of the ring. They appeared to be no more than piles of sawdust, and then—they struck."

Doctor Hopper laced up his shoe once more. "But why did they seize Miss Juliana? Of what possible use could a bareback-riding butterfly be to them?"

"Of inhuman use, so cruel as to compare to nothing we've ever dealt with before." Mantis put up the collar of his cloak against the damp wind. "Let us hurry, Doctor, before the threads of this case are blown away by the winds of time."

· · ·

A carriage clicked its way along through that part of the city where strangers are neither welcome nor safe. In every doorway dangerous figures lurked, and on every corner there were signs of evil omen. When the carriage stopped, it was a cautious Doctor Hopper who stepped down.

(7)

"I take it, Mantis, that it's absolutely essential for us to be here?" Doctor Hopper looked nervously around him.

"I am well-known at this café—" Mantis pointed with the stem of his pipe. "—and no one shall trouble us."

Doctor Hopper took a solid grip on his cane, and entered the café with Mantis. On all sides, daggers gleamed, but Mantis made his way calmly through the crowd, choosing a table in the corner of the room. "Make yourself comfortable, Doctor, for I believe we shall have to be here for awhile."

"I don't like this place, Mantis." Doctor Hopper sat down, careful first to touch his wallet, to see that it had not been picked already.

"An indecent lot," said Mantis, coldly eyeing the deadly assortment of characters at the other tables. "But useful."

Through two swinging doors at the kitchen, a waiter emerged, his several arms bearing numerous steaming dishes and drinks, which he distributed to the hungry, muttering crowd. Then, turning, he slithered toward the most recently occupied table.

"Good evening, Inspector." His false, shallow smile fell on Mantis. "And what brings you here tonight? Usually it means you are in search of someone."

"Usually." Inspector Mantis rubbed the ashen bowl of his pipe. "Bring us two cups of rose nectar and a plate of bee-bread."

The waiter withdrew with a sinister glide, and Doctor Hopper stared across the table at his lean, bony friend. "How can you eat in a den like this, Mantis? I'm appalled . . ."

"We have a long night ahead of us, Doctor. And if I'm not mistaken, it will carry us far afield. You'd be wise to eat while you can."

The fog beyond the café window turned to a faint drizzle, and the crowd came and went, while the lamps burned on. Inspector Mantis, after touching a few morsels of the food, fell into a deep meditation, and Doctor Hopper finally allowed himself to eat the entire dish of beebread. "But dash it all, Mantis, are we to stay here forever?" He looked at his apparently rigid companion.

"No," said Mantis, as if suddenly waking, "for there is our thread—" He nodded toward the door, where a vicious-looking tick had just entered, carrying a heavy satchel.

"And what treacherous profession is he practicing, I wonder?" asked Doctor Hopper, following the tick's stealthy progress through the shadows.

"He is a seller of poisons, Doctor, whose names I'm sure would be familiar to you."

"Poisons? Well, this is the place for it, I must say."

"Indeed," said Mantis, "and that is why we are here."

"But what have poisons to do with Miss Juliana Butterfly?"

"Everything, my dear Hopper. Simply everything." Inspector Mantis leaned his elbows on the table and regarded the poison-seller's approach with interest. The tick was doing a lively business, handing out numerous corked vials of his noxious wares, for which he received payment in good measure from the unwholesome inhabitants of the café.

"You there." Mantis spoke with cool indifference.

The tick turned. "Let the buyer beware—" He sidled closer to the table, and laid his black bag down in front of Mantis. "—for what I sell is lethal."

"Have you—" Mantis leaned toward him. "—hydrogen cyanide?"

"Newly added to my line." The tick smiled and dug into his bag, then placed a shining little vial on the table. "Will there by anything else?" he asked, still smiling, his eyes gleaming as he took payment from the inspector.

"I should like a heart poison, if you have one."

"Certainly—" The tick rummaged in his bag again, and placed another bright little bottle down. "A most powerful cardenolide. You could kill a horse with it."

Doctor Hopper shifted uncomfortably in his chair. The poison-seller gave off an unpleasant odor, to which was added the further unpleasantness of his deadly wares, now glittering brightly on the table. And Mantis still wasn't done with his purchases!

"—strychnine," said the inspector. "Do you have it?"

"Another new addition—" The tick went into his bag again. "You've caught me at a good time." The third gleaming vial was set on the table.

"Excellent," said Inspector Mantis, placing all three vials in his cloak. "These are just what I've been looking for."

"Should you have need of more, you can find me here." The tick wrapped his black cape around himself, and moved off through the crowd, toward the door.

"Now then, Doctor," said Mantis, standing quickly, "the chase is on."

He and Hopper hurried out of the café, into the drizzling rain, in time to see the tick alighting to a carriage. Mantis raised a long arm, signaling another cab, and instructed the driver to follow.

"But what is the connection, Mantis?" Doctor Hopper sank into the carriage seat, shaking the rain off his derby. "How does this poison-selling tick link us to Miss Juliana Butterfly?"

"Defenseless butterflies," murmured Inspector Mantis, almost as if to himself.

"Yes, exactly," said Doctor Hopper quickly. "Poor defenseless creatures being preyed upon by—by whom?"

"But are they defenseless, Doctor?" Mantis sat up sharply. "Think—what is the butterfly's defense?"

"Why—" Doctor Hopper tapped himself lightly on the forehead with his cane as he thought for a moment. "—I suppose it's those big bright eyes butterflies have painted on their wings. They look like the eyes of a hawk, or a cat, or some such creature, and birds who might eat the butterflies are frightened off. Am I correct?"

"Yes," said Mantis, "but there is still another defense, connected with—"

"Poison! By Jove, Mantis—" Hopper struck himself on the head with his cane again, to the point of nearly knocking himself unconscious, but he hardly noticed, so great was his excitement. "Butterflies contain poison in their bodies—making them very unappetizing morsels to the birds! That's it!"

"Yes, Doctor, that is precisely it. And those three poisons are—"

"Cyanide, cardenolide, and strychnine."

"Which the tick in the carriage ahead of us has for sale." Mantis leaned his head discreetly out the window. "His little evening's work is done, I think, and his bag is empty."

The tick's carriage was stopping, and Mantis and Hopper hid their faces as their own coach slowly passed by. The tick was descending, black cape flowing; he stepped into the street and quickly disappeared into a dark row of buildings.

Mantis tapped on his driver's window, and was already climbing down as the carriage stopped, Doctor Hopper following him, into a neighborhood little better than the one they'd come from. The air was filled with menace; the fog, which had once again set in, cloaked the street. *"This way,"* said Inspector Mantis softly, and Doctor Hopper moved with him, through a narrow passage between the buildings. Water dripped from a rain gutter somewhere above them, but there was no other noise on either side. Mantis pointed downward, to the faint imprint of a footstep left by the tick. More footprints led through the passageway and out the other side, into a large courtyard.

It was empty, lit by a single lamp which threw a feeble glow through the smoke-like haze. Doctor Hopper wrinkled up his nose. "I say, Mantis," he remarked in a whisper, "what is that loathsome smell?"

"It is the trail, Doctor."

Mantis moved swiftly across the courtyard, pausing only a moment to sniff the air. Doctor Hopper sniffed with him, recalling that the poison-seller had given off the same odor, but weaker, and less disgusting. What could be the source of such a dreadful stench?

"Behold," said Mantis, indicating the nameplate on the door directly before them, on which was written

A. Stinkbug, Esquire

"Must we—?" Doctor Hopper was reaching for a handkerchief to cover his nose, when Mantis quickly threw out a long arm and pressed them both back into the shadows of the building.

The door opened, and the poison-seller came out, his bag heavy once again. They watched him pass through the vaporous glow of the courtyard and when his footsteps had faded out of earshot, Inspector Mantis bent low beside a window. With a long slender tool from his pocket-kit, he slipped the window latch, and carefully, noiselessly, raised the glass.

An overwhelming odor struck them. Doctor Hopper reeled back, nearly fainting; Inspector Mantis clutched his arm and drew him through the window, as the good doctor struggled again to get a handkerchief to his nose.

"*Gad, what a place.*" Hopper staggered forward through malodorous clouds that seemed to come from the very walls.

"*He is ahead of us . . .*" Mantis indicated a crack of light coming from beneath a door.

The doctor supported himself weakly with his cane, as Mantis turned the knob. The door creaked open, and beyond it, sitting in the middle of the room was A. Stinkbug, dining on a dish of cabbage.

"Who are you?" he asked, looking up suspiciously, with the spoon halfway to his lip.

The smell, whether from the cabbage, or Stinkbug himself, was impossible to bear. Doctor Hopper sank against the back of a chair, holding his head. Inspector Mantis, swaying dizzily, managed to speak. "It is we who should ask that question of you."

"I? I am A. Stinkbug."

"A purveyor of poisons," snapped Mantis, his eyes watering from the smell.

"You look pale, sir," said A. Stinkbug. "May I offer you a drop of something to revive you?" Stinkbug pointed to a stoppered bottle.

"A drop indeed!" Mantis dizzily gripped the edge of

the table, his gaze upon the evil-looking liquid in the bottle.

"Two drops, perhaps, for one as tall as you," smiled Stinkbug.

"I fear—" Mantis took a step backward, his long legs beginning to buckle beneath him. "—we must withdraw." He lifted Doctor Hopper from the chair the doctor had collapsed in, and assisted him toward the door.

"Leaving so soon?" Stinkbug rose from his seat. "But I thought you came to talk about poisons."

"Another time, perhaps." Mantis, coughing and choking, dragged the half-unconscious doctor out.

Stinkbug laughed. "Did my little home offend you in some way? You seem to be holding your nose."

Mantis and Hopper fumbled at the outer door and tumbled drunkenly into the courtyard. Stinkbug slammed the door behind them, and they breathed deeply in the cool night air, recovering their wits.

"Upon my soul," said Doctor Hopper, "that was a nauseating encounter. And we learned not a thing."

"On the contrary, Doctor," said Mantis. "We now know where Miss Juliana Butterfly is."

"We do?" Hopper stared up at his companion, mustache ends twitching with surprise.

"Yes, Doctor, we do. The courtyard, and the house, were scattered with tiny clues. Here is one such—" Inspector Mantis handed a tiny sprig of green to Doctor Hopper.

"Eh? What's this?"

"It is an herb, Doctor, called thyme. Whoever brings the shipments of poison to Stinkbug comes from a place overgrown with thyme."

"I see," said Doctor Hopper, putting on his eyeglasses and examining the sprig of thyme more closely.

"You'll notice," continued Mantis, "bits of dry, sandy soil clinging to the herb."

"Yes, quite right."

"We have both seen such soil as that, Doctor, in the ruined vineyards of Old Grapeleaf, which lies to the south of us. It is a most desolate area, forbidding and austere."

"And you think that's where Miss Juliana Butterfly is held captive?"

"I'm certain of it. Look, Doctor, with my magnifying glass—" Mantis took out his lens and handed it to Hopper. "Do you see those glittering bits of color mixed with the sand?"

"I do."

"They are the scales from a butterfly's wings."

"Why—so they are!" The doctor looked up, his eyes filled with excitement.

Mantis smiled. "Our host, A. Stinkbug, Esquire, thought his game was completely concealed. But those tiny glittering bits of color were everywhere in his house—on the tablecloth, on the rug, and some, I don't doubt, floating in his cabbage soup."

"But this is extraordinary, Mantis! You've solved the case!"

"Hardly, Doctor. For now we must go and grapple with the fiend of the ruined vineyards, an adversary more powerful than any we have ever faced."

"Who is—?" The doctor removed his glasses, an anxious question written in his eyes.

"The Tarantula," said Inspector Mantis, and once again his long arms locked behind his back.

Thus, in silence, the two friends marched along, only their footsteps echoing in the shrouded street, as they hastened toward the next square in the game, a dark and dangerous one, where terrible forces lurked.

. . .

The train rumbled through the night. Doctor Hopper, asleep in his seat, rocked back and forth against the window. Beside him, a traveling chess board on his lap, Inspector Mantis amused himself, his mind never happy unless it was engaged in some problem of pursuit. He prepared to move his knight, to make the final capture of the enemy king, when the train whistle sounded, the carriage jerked, and the pieces fell off the board, onto his cloak.

"Well, well, Doctor—" He gathered up the fallen combatants and tucked them back into their little box. "—it seems we have arrived."

"Eh?" Doctor Hopper looked up sleepily, then stretched and stood. "I was dreaming—of Miss Juliana Butterfly."

Inspector Mantis stepped into the aisle. "And what was she doing, pray tell?"

"Performing bareback again, on her prancing horsefly."

"Let us hope that will be the outcome," said Mantis, as they descended the steps of the train, onto the station platform. "But I fear it is a nightmare that awaits us, rather than a dream."

"I would risk anything for Miss Juliana," said Doctor Hopper resolutely.

"Then I shall ask you to make immediate inquiry of the nearest buyer and seller of gold, as to whether any amount of that precious substance has come his way lately, and if so, from whom. Meet me here at the station in an hour."

"And where are you off to, Mantis?"

But the inspector was already on his way, calling back over his shoulder, "*Hurry, Doctor, for the life of Miss Juliana is at stake!*"

Doctor Hopper moved off as quickly as his hopping legs would carry him. In very little time he found the sign of the *Golden Scarab*, and entered the seller's shop.

The Scarab, seated at a pair of scales, looked up. "May I help you?"

"Is that gold dust you are weighing, sir?" asked the doctor.

"Are you buying or selling?" snapped the Scarab.

"Neither."

"Then don't waste my time." The Scarab went back to studying his scales.

Doctor Hopper placed his hat and cane on the counter. "Well, perhaps I am interested." He pointed at the dust. "Where is this mined?"

"That," said the Scarab, "is none of your business."

The door swung open behind him, but Doctor Hopper pretended not to notice; instead he bent over a display case of golden coins, as if examining them carefully. But from the corner of his eye, he watched a pair of legs come into view, their shape obliterated by clinging bits of sawdust, sand, and sprigs of thyme.

The Scarab's voice rose in greeting. "And how are you this evening?"

Doctor Hopper raised his eyes a little more, and saw a bug whose entire wardrobe was formed of clinging debris. "I've come to sell," said the shabby creature in a harsh, low tone, as he dropped a heavy bag on the Scarab's counter.

"You've come to the right place," said the Scarab, putting the bag on his scales. "Did you have a good trip?"

The slovenly bug pointed to bits of mud and river weed that were stuck to his sleeve. "The road is bad. The bridge was nearly washed away, and me with it."

"Bridge washed out?" Doctor Hopper looked up casually from the display case. "And where is that? I wouldn't want to run into it."

"Bitter Rot Road," scowled the bug. "Where it forks to the right." He picked at his disgusting sleeve again. "I've ruined a perfectly good suit."

"Thank you," said Hopper, as he withdrew toward the door. "I shall be on the watch."

Now, by George, I must hurry!

The street flew beneath his feet as he rushed back toward the railroad station. Before he'd reached it, a carriage pulled in beside him and Inspector Mantis leaned down from it, pulling him in.

"Ah, Mantis, I have found someone selling gold—"

"From Bitter Rot Road," said Mantis quietly, "beyond the river."

"Was it a dust-covered bug revealed it to you?"

"The Assassin Gang is everywhere in this unfortunate city, Doctor, their bodies cloaked with trash, their conscience covered in crime. But they are only intermediaries. Our real quarry is ahead of us." He pointed with his pipe, as the carriage swung out of the city, onto a road lined with dead, rotted grapevines, their branches hanging sad and bare. The carriage bounced and rattled along over the ill-kept road, axles creaking ominously.

"There," said Mantis, "the road forks."

"And there is the bridge."

The driver opened his window and spoke down to them. "I'll not risk crossing that." He pointed with his whip at the teetering bridge.

Inspector Mantis opened the carriage door. "We must proceed on foot, Doctor. But our enemy cannot be far off. Look what grows among the vines."

"Thyme," said the doctor, picking off a sprig.

The driver of the carriage called down to them. "Who is it you seek out here?"

"The Tarantula," said Inspector Mantis.

The driver yanked his carriage around, whipped his steeds, and rattled away in a cloud of dust.

"Stout fellow," said Mantis, stepping onto the swaying bridge.

"A rotter," said Doctor Hopper, gripping his hat brim and balancing himself with his cane.

Mantis gave his companion a sly glance. "Perhaps—" The inspector stepped gingerly over a jagged broken timber. "—he's never seen Miss Juliana Butterfly perform."

"Then he has missed the greatest sight of a lifetime," said Doctor Hopper.

Together they made their way over the rickety bridge, every stick of it swaying now, as the swollen stream knocked it about

No sooner had Mantis and Hopper set foot on the far shore than the whole bridge was swept away like matchsticks on the water.

"Well," said Mantis, "now our way is clear. There can be no retreat."

"So much the worse for the Tarantula," said Doctor Hopper, swinging his cane.

Mantis touched Hopper lightly on the back of the neck. "If he stings the cervical ganglia, you are finished."

Doctor Hopper paled slightly, but his voice did not waver. "If he is holding Miss Juliana Butterfly captive, he must answer to me."

Inspector Mantis swept his eyes over the hillside beyond them. "The ground is dry and pebbly. The Tarantula's underground manor is near."

The two friends paused then, as Inspector Mantis began a more careful sweep of the terrain. ". . . yes . . . yes, over there . . . and there . . ."

"Confound it, Mantis, what do you see? I can't make out anything."

Mantis laid a hand on Hopper's shoulder and pointed him first in one direction, then another. "Do you see? A beetle's leg here, the wing of a bee over there . . ."

"Ah! And there, how ghastly—"

A dragonfly's head, baked by the sun, stared at them from the middle of the field. They moved forward with cautious steps. All around them, in every direction, it was barren as the moon, save for indigestible bits of leg and wing the Tarantula had dumped out of its underground home.

"There, Hopper, there is the entrance—" Mantis pointed to a turret rising out of the earth, decorated by dragonfly skulls. Doctor Hopper swallowed with some difficulty, his knees beginning to tremble.

"But," continued Mantis, "we cannot hope to defeat him in his tunnel. He is absolute master there. Every twist and turn is known to him, and the walls are lined with webbing up which he can travel like lightning but in which we would be mired."

"But what shall we do then?" asked Doctor Hopper.

"We must lure him out," said Mantis.

"An excellent idea," said Hopper, his knees ceasing to tremble. "How shall we do it?"

"You must climb the turret, Doctor, and play your violin. He will hear it and come after you."

"Mantis, I say—"

"Miss Juliana Butterfly is somewhere in there." Mantis pointed to the dark opening of the turret, and Doctor Hopper sighed, shrugged his shoulders, and walked, knees trembling again, toward the Tarantula's manor.

At the base of the turret he paused, and looked back toward Mantis, but the inspector had already disappeared. Hopper braced himself, held his hat, and hopped in one bound to the top of the turret.

There, he began to play, as if to the setting sun, but his coattails were hanging into the dark terrible hole, and his elbows were resting on hollow dragonfly heads. He wished very much to be back at home, sitting in front of a cheerful fire, popping popcorn. But then he thought of Miss Juliana, held prisoner somewhere down in the darkness, and he played louder, and more sweetly, as if playing to her.

Suddenly four eyes gleamed in the darkness, and then a huge shadow skimmed up the silken walls. Doctor Hopper leapt off the turret, dragonfly heads tumbling with him. He landed lightly and turned to defend himself. He was a foot-fighter of some skill; he locked his legs for a swift kick. The sun was blotted out by a great hairy body sailing down through the air toward him. Four malevolent eyes glittered and two glistening fangs went for his neck.

He dodged, and kicked into the monster's stomach, but the Tarantula only laughed, as the kick landed harmlessly against its chest armor.

"What a foolish fiddler you are." The Tarantula went for the doctor's jugular vein. The nimble doctor dodged once more, and the Tarantula pursued him, laughing. "You think you can escape me? You're mine now, little fellow." The Tarantula's poison fangs opened again, but just as they did so, a long green saw-toothed arm closed around his hairy neck.

"Mantis, thank goodness . . ." Doctor Hopper hopped out of harm's way, the Tarantula held back by the powerful grip of Inspector Mantis.

The Tarantula struggled against the inspector's iron grasp. He rolled, and Mantis went beneath him, but his grip didn't loosen.

"That's it!" shouted Doctor Hopper, hopping about excitedly. "You've got him! Here I come, Mantis!" The doctor leapt in with his cane, trying to knock the Tarantula out.

A hairy leg tripped him, and a dripping fang stuck him

"You're mine now, little fellow."

through the shirt front, into his chest. The barren landscape suddenly went round. The struggling figures before him became a blur; he staggered backward, pain shooting through his body, then stumbled forward again, trying to enter the battle once more. Feebly, he struck with his cane.

". . . you've got . . . him, Mantis . . . don't . . . let go . . ."

Sand and gravel flew about, as Mantis and his opponent whirled in the dust. The Tarantula's swift legs kicked out in all directions, and his hideous fangs snapped at the sky, poison shining on the needle tips. His monstrous body sprung upward in the air, convulsed by murderous passion, but when he dropped down Mantis still clung to the throat, his own body in some dark trance of concentrated power. Hopper had seen such battles before; once those forearms of Mantis's had locked, no force could open them, not even a machine of death like the Tarantula, whose legs were kicking less fiercely now. The spider's glittering eyes fluttered, as the vice-like grip of the inspector tightened ever tighter on the hairy throat. A moment more, and the Tarantula collapsed, unconscious on the ground.

"Quickly, Doctor!" Handcuffs flashed, and they set to shackling the monster. Hopper's hands trembled with the iron cuffs, his arms cold and aching, but he managed to close the links around the legs of the hairy fiend.

Mantis's own cuffs clicked shut, and he stepped back from their still-unconscious prisoner. "That should do it. Let us enter the dungeon."

Wearily, Doctor Hopper followed Inspector Mantis over the top of the turret and into the dark hole. Carefully, they picked their way down the wall, avoiding the network of sticky threads. The subterranean chamber went deep into the earth; Doctor Hopper's vision was blurred, his legs weak, but he groped his way along beside Mantis, through the ghastly labyrinth. Imprisoned fireflies provided the light, and monstrous trophies covered the silken walls. At every turning there was evidence of some new outrage perpetrated against the citizens of the fields and hills surrounding the manor—beetlehorn furniture, fly-wing drapes, fur rugs made out of bumblebees.

I shan't live to see the end of it, thought Doctor Hopper, feeling the poison spreading slowly through his veins. The Tarantula's fang had missed the cervical ganglia, but had nonetheless penetrated deeply, and the doctor knew—he was doomed.

But he held on, wanting to see Miss Juliana safe and out of this terrible place.

"There, Hopper," said Inspector Mantis, "that barred door—"

"Yes," said Hopper weakly. "Let us open it, quickly."

They lifted the beam that held it, swung it open, and then stared in amazement at the saddest sight either of them had ever seen—dozens of butterflies, chained to the walls, their wings naked and bare.

"They've been stripped of their gold!" cried the doctor, aghast.

"Yes," said Mantis, "it is as I feared."

"How foul," stammered the doctor. "An unspeakable crime."

"*Help us,*" cried the butterflies. "*Loosen our chains . . .*"

"At once," said Doctor Hopper, and went to the only butterfly in the room who had not yet been violated. "Miss Juliana . . ."

He removed his derby and bowed before
the imprisoned beauty. Then, with hands
that were growing more numb every
second, he freed her from her chains.

"*Oh thank you, thank you,*" sobbed
Miss Juliana, falling into his arms.
"I was to be next. My wings were
to be stripped this night."

"It shall never happen, dear
lady," said the doctor, attempting
to smile. But the poison had
spread to his neck, his face,
his entire body. He swayed
before her, then stumbled
backward, and collapsed.

"Doctor . . ." Mantis
rushed to his side.

"It's nothing . . ." Hopper
looked up weakly, still trying to
smile. It was most embarrassing to be
dying this way, in front of Miss Juliana. "The
Tarantula . . . gave me . . . a glancing wound . . ."

"There's no such thing as a glancing wound with
a tarantula," said Mantis, hurrying the doctor to his feet.

The other butterflies were now freeing each other, and one
of them spoke up. "I heard the Tarantula talking to the Assassin
Bugs one night, about the only antidote for his bite."

"Yes?" snapped Mantis. "And what is it?"

"The victim must dance."

"Yes, of course!" cried Mantis. "How could I have forgotten! The tarantella! The dance of the Tarantula! It is the only cure known . . ."

"Dance, Doctor!" cried the butterflies. "Dance with us!"

Hopper shook his head, but Mantis spoke in his ear. "You must. It will drive the poison from your system."

Hopper's fiddle had fallen to the floor and one of the butterflies picked it up and began to play.

"Dance with me, Doctor," said Miss Juliana, taking him into her arms.

The fiddling butterfly gave forth a tune in 6/8 time, and Miss Juliana spun the doctor around. He staggered with her, staring blankly into her iridescent eyes. His dream had come true, of seeing her safe, but as Mantis had said, a nightmare had awaited them too, and he was falling into it, into the nightmare of a chilled, poisoned heart.

But Miss Juliana held him up, her strong circus arms carrying his weight, and whirling him around to the tune, so that his heart somehow kept pumping, pumping life, and his legs kept moving though they seemed mired in lead.

"Dance, dance, dance, dance, dance, dance . . ." The butterflies called and clapped out the time, and Miss Juliana whispered it in his ear, so that the beating of the music became the beat of his heart, beating for her. His right leg suddenly twitched, shot through with life, and then his left one followed, twitching still more crazily.

"The poison is moving!" shouted Mantis. "Faster!"

The fiddler increased his tempo, and Hopper's legs went into spasm, kicking as if by themselves, as Miss Juliana whirled him to the mad rhythm of the tarantella. The sweat poured from his brow in bitter streams of poison that dripped into his shirt collar, poisoning him no more.

He felt a lightness returning to his limbs, felt his heart responding, as Miss Juliana whispered, *"You dance divinely, Doctor . . ."*

"Oh, not really, I'm just . . . hopping about . . ." But he was gliding now, the poison thinned out inside him, and his strength coming back.

He turned with her, clicking his heels, as the fiddle went into a racing finish, faster and faster and faster. His legs followed, kicking the last of the poison away, and the butterflies shouted "Hurrah!" and lifted him onto their shoulders.

"Here now, I say . . ."

They carried him out of the dungeon, and through the dark winding tunnel, into the light of day once more.

. . .

P. T. Barnworm escorted Doctor Hopper and Inspector Mantis to a ringside seat. "Gentlemen, you have a free pass to this circus for life."

Mantis and Hopper sat down, popcorn on their laps, and cotton candy in their hands. A balloon was attached to the doctor's derby. "Well," he said, "I hope Miss Juliana has recovered."

"Entirely," said P. T. Barnworm. "The few flecks of gold she lost from her wings have grown back."

"Do my eyes deceive me," said Inspector Mantis, "or is that the lady in question, coming toward us now?"

P. T. Barnworm extended his arm toward Miss Juliana. "Your friends have come to see you."

"I was hoping you would," said Miss Juliana, her costume glittering brightly as she joined them at the front row. "Did you know—" She raised her head toward the trapeze above, where a brilliantly robed performer was waiting to take the bar. "—I'm going to be married."

"Congratulations . . ." Inspector Mantis put his cotton candy down and shook Miss Juliana's hand. Doctor Hopper shook it too, but his voice was hardly more than a whisper. "May you enjoy every happiness . . ."

The horseflies came trotting out at that moment, and Miss Juliana leapt gracefully upward, straddling two of them at once, and they carried her away, to the cracking of P. T. Barnworm's whip.

Inspector Mantis looked at his friend. "Did I detect something in your voice just now when Miss Juliana informed us of—"

"Bosh," said Doctor Hopper. "Don't be absurd."

"I see," said Mantis.

Miss Juliana circled by on her prancing steeds, her radiant wings floating out behind her.

"She is a friend, no more than that," said Doctor Hopper, as she went by.

"You have cotton candy in your mustache," said Mantis.

THE CASE OF
The Frightened Scholar

IN A LITTLE FLAT on Flea Street, the fire burned low in the fireplace, and a recently-used popcorn popper rested on the hearth. In an armchair beside the hearth, Doctor Hopper slept contentedly, hands folded in his lap, bits of popcorn scattered over his vest and trousers.

On the other side of the room, Inspector Mantis was engaged in the throwing of some darts; it was a particularly difficult shot, three darts held in one hand. He bent his arm, aimed, and threw at the target on the wall. One dart went into the footstool, another went into the back of the sofa, and the third imbedded itself in the door—just as a knock came on the other side.

I sincerely hope, said Mantis to himself, quickly gathering up his darts, *that isn't our landlady. She wouldn't approve of darts in her door, not at all.* He shook Hopper awake. "Straighten up your popper, Doctor. It might be Mrs Inchworm."

"Come now, Mantis," said Hopper peevishly, "we *live* here,

don't we? Shouldn't a person be allowed to pop a little popcorn without immediately cleaning up? I mean, where's the joy of the thing if one must be constantly cleaning up . . ."

The knock came again, and Mantis hurried toward it. "I'm coming, Mrs Inchworm . . ."

He opened the door with a ceremonious bow. A bedbug was looking back at him, nightcap in hand.

"Inspector Mantis?"

"Indeed, sir," said Mantis, much relieved. "What can we do for you?"

The bedbug yawned, twisting his nightcap around in his hand. "I've been sent by my employer."

"And who, might I ask, is your employer?"

"Professor Channing Booklouse."

"And what is Professor Booklouse's problem?"

"He shall have to tell you himself." The bedbug blinked sleepily and pointed toward the window, and the street below. "I have a carriage waiting."

Mantis went to the coatrack and donned his long cloak, then hustled Doctor Hopper from his chair. "Come, Doctor. The game is at hand once more."

"Oh rot," said Hopper, clamping on his derby hat and stuffing himself into his coat, as bits of popcorn fell from his vest onto the rug. He was filled with butter and salt and wanted nothing more than to enjoy a quiet evening by the fire —but instead, Mantis was dragging him off to what would un- doubtedly prove to be another wild, bizarre, and most likely dangerous night's work.

. . .

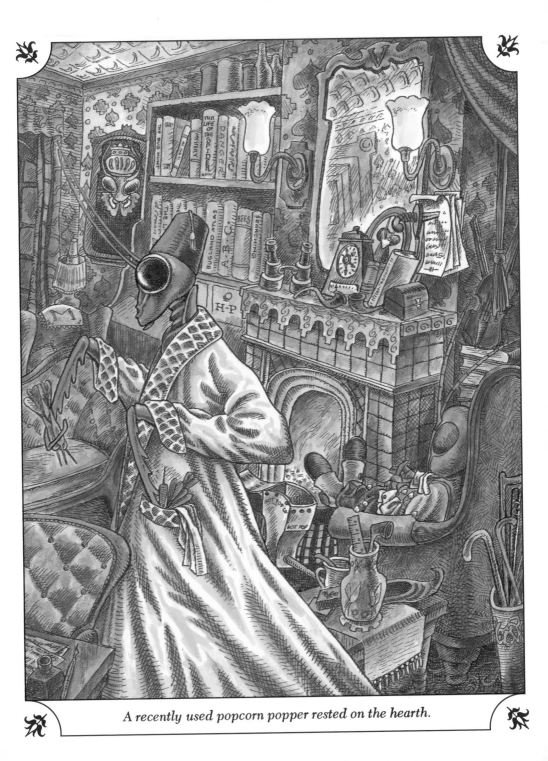

A recently used popcorn popper rested on the hearth.

The carriage wheels slowed, then stopped, and the bedbug stepped down, the tail of his nightshirt appearing under his coat. "We're here," he said, and Mantis and Hopper followed, to the sidewalk. The street was an ordinary one, of orderly little houses piled so close together the fog could barely creep between them. The bedbug opened a rickety gate and pointed the way across an untended bit of lawn, toward a house in which but a single lamp burned.

"I see Professor Booklouse has been troubled by prowlers," said Mantis.

The bedbug's head turned quickly, but Mantis merely pointed toward the newly installed window guards. The sudden growling of a dogfly from within the house seemed to confirm the supposition, for the bedbug hopped backward at the sound of it. "A new dog," he said, taking out his keys and fumbling with them, as the dogfly continued to make a ferocious racket.

"Be careful, he bites," said the bedbug, swinging open the door. "Back! Get back there, you!"

The bedbug kicked at the dogfly, and his bedroom slipper flew off. The dogfly withdrew with the slipper in his teeth. Nevertheless, Doctor Hopper gave the beast a wide berth. His trousers were not exactly new, but he could do without some vicious mongrel chewing on them.

"This way," said the bedbug. One slipper on and one off, he led them through a dark musty hallway, toward the only room where a light was showing. "Right through there . . ."

Professor Booklouse rose to greet them. He was a timid little scholar with spectacles on the end of his nose and papers and books scattered about him. "I'm so grateful to you for coming," he said, looking over the tops of his spectacles toward Mantis and Hopper. "Won't you please sit down? May I get you something? A drop of nectar, perhaps?"

"Your story, sir," said Mantis, seating himself, "will be refreshment enough."

Doctor Hopper harumphed. He could have done with a drop of nectar on a wet night like this, but Mantis, confound him, had no concern for anything the slightest bit comforting once he was on a case. Hopper resigned himself to little in the way of pleasure this night, and sank into a battered old armchair, to listen to the tale of Professor Channing Booklouse, who was now pacing, voice trembling as he spoke.

"I'm a quiet sort, Mr Mantis, who's never given anyone cause for worry or trouble. I live here, with my books, and my work." The troubled scholar turned, gesturing toward the walls of his room, which were a solid mass of bookshelves from floor to ceiling. "I've nibbled my way through thousands of volumes, digesting what I could of my subject—"

"Which is?"

"The History of Bugland, from its earliest beginnings." The

scholar forced a little smile. "It's not a subject everyone would find enjoyable, but to me it's been a life's work. Only now—" He gripped the edge of his table, and Doctor Hopper could see that he'd begun to shake all over.

"Yes," said Mantis, "please go on, Professor Booklouse."

"Only now, my life has been threatened." Booklouse went white; he attempted to push his spectacles up on his nose, but his trembling hand could barely find the rims. "Oh dear, oh dear, if only I hadn't come upon that book—"

"What book, Professor Booklouse?" Mantis leaned forward, speaking softly.

"The book that has caused all this trouble." Booklouse flopped down at his desk and put his head in his hands. His assistant, the bedbug, spoke from his corner of the room, in a reclining chair. Both his slippers were now off, and his night-cap was down over his eyes. His voice came in a sleepy whisper. "Professor Booklouse . . . found a book . . . quite by accident . . ."

The trembling professor raised his head from his desk, knocking against a hanging lamp, which danced, casting moving shadows on the wall, that seemed to tell a story of their own, of fright and capture. "Yes, yes, quite by accident. I came upon it stuffed in a flowerbox in the Gypsy Moth Tea Room, not far from here. Are you familiar with it?"

"I'm afraid not."

"It's a pleasant little place, with a delicious menu. I usually eat a few pages whenever I go there. The glue on the menu is, I might say, outstanding."

Mantis sighed in his chair, waiting for the more useful facts to emerge from Booklouse's nervous narrative.

"Well, on this particular day," continued the professor, "I was on my way out of the Tea Room, feeling quite stuffed." He smiled sheepishly. "You see, I'd eaten the entire dessert page—"

"Get on with it, Booklouse, if you would, please."

"Yes, yes of course, forgive me. I was going out the door, when I noticed something concealed in one of the flowerboxes. I withdrew it and much to my surprise found it to be an early *Illustrated History of Bugland*. I took it home, and that evening I devoured its contents. There, on the edge of my desk, is all that remains of it."

Mantis reached for the volume, which consisted now of only the front and back cover. Professor Booklouse spoke again. "It was a tasty little work, and I considered myself very lucky to have found it, until—" Here Booklouse broke off, his body beginning to tremble again, and his spectacles slipped down his nose once more.

"Yes, Professor?" said Mantis. "Please continue."

"Well," said Booklouse, trying to control his emotions, "soon after I'd digested it, I realized that it had been more than just a history of Bugland."

"And how was that?"

"I began to have the strangest information at my fingertips—not about the history of Bugland, but instead . . ." The timorous scholar seemed to pale to his roots. He looked quickly toward his barred window, then back toward his guests, as his voice

(41)

went low. ". . . instead, I had somehow thoroughly digested the most secret information about the highest workings in the Admiralty!"

Doctor Hopper sat straight up, and looked directly at Mantis. "This is most serious."

"Indeed it is," said Mantis, again opening the covers of the devoured book. "You say you ate every page of it?"

"To the last scrap," said Booklouse. "It was, after all, my special subject. Or so I thought."

"Until you began to have certain knowledge of naval matters—"

"Naval, yes! And of the secret affairs of the Embassy!" Professor Booklouse stood, knocking his head on the lamp again, setting it swinging once more.

From the corner of the room, low snores broke forth from the bedbug. Mantis stared thoughtfully at the remains of the *Illustrated History*, as the lamp swung back and forth above it. "Obviously, the book was coded."

"Yes!" exclaimed the scholar. "And whoever coded it was a spy. And that spy now means to take my life!"

"Or wants his book back."

"But I've eaten it!" cried the terrified professor. He gestured once again toward his library shelves. "As I have eaten every other volume I own.

"There are the empty covers. The contents have all been chewed over thoroughly, night in and night out, until nothing is left. My research has been complete, including the volume you hold in your hand, which I wish I'd never seen. Oh dear, oh dear . . ."

"Have you contacted anyone in our government since this happened?"

"No, I've been afraid to do anything, except contact you."

"I suggest you maintain that position for now, and leave matters in our hands. Doctor Hopper, if you'd care to join me, I'm going to have a look around the garden."

Mantis stood, and with Doctor Hopper, proceeded out through the hall, and onto the porch. The inspector's glance went quickly over things there, and he stepped into the garden, where his curiosity seemed to be satisfied just as quickly. A final step took him into the street, where he bent for a moment over some faint impressions of a wheel, left in the mud. "There's nothing for us here, Doctor," he said, straightening up. "As might be expected, a spy is not likely to leave clear traces. We can only say he is long-legged, walks with a slight crouch, and has one boot worn down slightly at the heel. Not much to go on, really."

"Blast you, Mantis, and how did you know *that* much?" Hopper stared around the unkempt garden and the street, which revealed nothing to his searching eyes.

Mantis ignored the question, his mind already jumping forward to the next square. "Doctor, does my memory serve me correctly? Was not the Duchess of Doodlebug once a patient of yours?"

"I treated her for lumbago."

"Then you must prevail upon her, to get us an invitation to the next Embassy Ball."

. . .

The music was grand, the gathering fancy, and Doctor Hopper was faintly embarrassed by it all, especially with the Duchess of Doodlebug introducing him to everyone. It might be to some people's taste, all these chandeliers and polished floors and glittering tables, but he'd as soon be in front of his own fireplace with the old popper going and nothing to do but listen to the rain on the roof.

"Oh Doctor, you must meet Ambassador Cornbore. Ambassador, this is Doctor Hopper, who cured my lumbago . . ."

"How do you do," said Cornbore. "I say, would you mind having a look in my ear? Whenever I meet a medical man, I like his opinion. Do you see anything in there?"

"I have an unobstructed view." Hopper excused himself and took refuge behind a large potted plant. Through the leaves he could watch things and not have to meet any more bores like Cornbore.

The Duchess of Doodlebug, he noticed, had now collared

Mantis and was towing him around. Hopper was happy to see Mantis's discomfort. Serves the fellow right for dragging us here, but of course there is a higher purpose. We've come to find a spy—long-legged, walking with a crouch.

But no such figure was in sight.

He has to be a clever sort, reflected Hopper. And he has to have an accomplice somewhere in Bugland—an enemy agent who would have picked up the coded *History of Bugland* had not Professor Channing Booklouse found it first and devoured it.

"Ooooooooo, Doctor Hopper, there you are!" The Duchess of Doodlebug caught him off guard, from behind.

"Ah yes, Duchess, I was just studying the foliage of this remarkable plant."

"You must come along, Doctor, and be introduced to Baron Blowfly."

What an infernal nuisance, thought Hopper, but then he saw that Baron Blowfly was long-legged, and walked with a crouch. A prime suspect!

Hopper quickly looked toward the Baron's bootheel, but could discern nothing beyond the Baron's bright spurs. Nonetheless, thought Hopper, one must be thorough. "How-de-do," he said, still trying to catch a glimpse of a worn bootheel.

"And what—" asked the Baron with a withering stare, "—are you looking at?"

"I was noticing your handsome spurs. Are you fond of riding?"

The Baron's eyebrow raised. He seemed to regard Doctor Hopper as one who'd gone mad.

"I'm always curious about a person's footwear," said Hopper, tilting a little to the side. "Show me a person's footwear and I'll tell you what they eat for breakfast."

The Baron stared coldly at him. "What did you say your name was?"

"Hopper. I'm the Duchess of Doodlebug's medical advisor."

"And what have you advised her of lately?"

"Of the importance of proper diet—lots of popcorn, the perfect food."

"*Pop*-corn?" exclaimed the Baron. "Surely you're not serious."

"Never heard of the glorious attributes?" Hopper looked up at the Baron. "Why, I was reading of its importance only the other day in the *Illustrated History of Bugland*—" Hopper squinted, looking for the slightest trace of reaction from Blowfly, but the Baron, flinching not an eyelash, leaned in over the doctor and repeated loudly, in disbelief, "*Pop*-corn?"

He turned on his bootheels, and walked away.

Hopper hopped after him, bending down to look for the telltale edge of a worn heel, when he was tapped gently on the back. "Did you drop something, Doctor?"

He leapt up, ready to defend against the Duchess once more, but instead it was Mantis towering above him.

"Mantis, I was about to confirm a bootheel."

"Blowfly's not our spy."

"Are you certain of it?"

"His height is a centimeter over that of the individual who left his print in Professor Booklouse's garden."

"Well," said Hopper, "have we found anything then?"

"We've found the leak," said Mantis. "The Lord of the Admiralty is over there."

Hopper looked toward a jovial old ruffian dipping a cup into the nectar bowl. "Yes, what about him?"

"Admiral Water Strider is inclined to indulge himself in the heavenly beverage to the point of indiscretion. Whatever leaks there are in his navy, the Admiral himself has drilled."

"But with whom?"

Mantis was about to speak when a shrill voice bore down upon them. "Ooooooooooooo, Doctor," exclaimed the Duchess of Doodlebug, "you must meet my daughter."

"I'm afraid we haven't time, Duch—" Hopper swallowed his words, as the most beautiful creature he'd ever seen suddenly appeared from behind the Duchess.

The creature smiled and held out her hand. "I'm happy to meet you."

Doctor Hopper bowed over her fingertips. "The pleasure is all mine," he said, and looked up into her charming face. How intelligent she seemed! How poised, confident, and graceful, how—

"Forgive us," said Mantis, stepping in beside his companion, "but we have urgent business we must attend to."

The Duchess of Doodlebug snapped her fan at them. "But the evening has just begun! One of you must dance with Laura."

"Mother, if the gentlemen must leave—" Laura Doodlebug's

eyes lingered on Doctor Hopper, and he seemed to read in them an invitation, to join her at the nectar bowl. Blast Mantis, with his urgent business!

"Then," said Mantis, pulling at the doctor's coattails, "since you are so kind as to excuse us, we shall withdraw."

They turned, Mantis urging the doctor toward the door, but Hopper turned back, in time to see Baron Blowfly bowing to Laura Doodlebug, and escorting her to the dance floor. "Dash it all, Mantis," growled Hopper, "you might have given me two moments with the young lady."

"There is another chase awaits us, Doctor, in service of the Admiralty."

"Hang the Admiralty," said Hopper. "I was staring into the prettiest eyes in the room."

"Later, Doctor. On some quiet afternoon you may take Miss Doodlebug on your arm. But this night holds an adventure which won't wait."

The banded footmenbugs bowed at the embassy door, and Hopper and Mantis stepped out, into the echoing stone court-yard. As they passed between the gathered carriages, Mantis casually pointed to one of them. "Interesting, Doctor, how wheels tell their own story, exactly as do bootheels." He touched the scarred edge of the wheel. "This mark perfectly matches that left in the mud on the street where Professor Booklouse lives."

"Why, then, we have our spy!"

"This is an embassy carriage, Doctor. It is used by a number of different officials."

"Well, we've only to watch for each of them, until we see the long-legged, crouching chap."

"His name is Gallgnat, Doctor, and he has already flown the net."

. . .

"But how do we know this fellow Gallgnat is the spy?" asked Hopper. They were crossing a footbridge above a small canal, their voices falling away into the fog that rolled along the water.

"While you were waltzing with the Duchess, Doctor, I was in the embassy offices, making certain measurements. The floor beneath Gallgnat's desk bears traces of a worn bootheel, through which a nail protrudes, enough to make small, distinctive scratches, such as I found on Professor Booklouse's front porch. Moreover, the arrangement of his lamp and chair indicated a tall man, crouching at his desk. This habitual warp evidenced in the professor's garden, where the bushes had been only slightly parted overhead, though the length and depth of the footprint within them remained the same as on clearer ground. Only someone with a natural crouch could leave such a track."

"Mantis, you astound me!"

"Nonsense. The fact remains, Gallgnat has fled."

"And are we following him? This fog is so thick I don't know where I am anymore."

"We are intercepting him, Doctor, at his next rendezvous."

"Which is?"

"I cannot say for certain. His singular bootheel indicated the direction we now travel in. For the rest of it, I must try and detect him—with *these*." Mantis touched his slender antennae lightly, and worked them back and forth in the air. "Difficult . . ." he muttered to himself. ". . . most difficult . . ."

Hopper's own antennae twitched and searched, but a million signals crossed the night, making an immense scramble of pulsations.

Mantis walked on, still muttering to himself, as his feelers moved left, right, left again. ". . . a few longitudinal veins . . . single cross vein . . . medial unbranched fold . . ."

Hopper shook his head in wonder. Mantis had the signal, his figure concentrating itself in a way familiar to the doctor. They'd be tracking now, to the bowels of the earth if need be, with no stopping for rest, nor for water should they find themselves dying of thirst in a desert. Mantis was unbalanced that way, a regular fiend for the chase, a mad dog actually, once he got the scent. Well, sighed Hopper, I'll get no sleep tonight.

Mantis led on, through a narrow cobble street that twisted and turned between century-old houses and then spilled out into a great open thoroughfare, which they crossed, only to plunge once more into a back alley time had forgotten. The footing was muddy, the lighting primitive, feeble flickering lamps doing little to penetrate the heavy mist, but Mantis tracked, his body hunched over, his head forward, until he himself must look like his long-legged, crouching prey, the traitorous Gallgnat.

Suddenly Hopper's own antennae twitched again. He paused, and swept them across the million-fold network of the night. Somewhere near, in the fog, was a popcorn wagon! "I say, Mantis—"

But the inspector was already turning, down a dark, dank passageway between two factory buildings, and the lovely popping signal faded. Hopper shuffled along in pursuit of his now swiftly-moving companion.

"*There*—" Mantis pointed to the track of a bootheel, worn slightly, with the outline of a nailhead in the corner. The inspector knelt, examining the bootheel. "Curses, Hopper, this track is two hours old."

"But how can you tell?"

"The toe has filled with water. The edges of the sole have crumbled. He's out beyond us again."

"Well, let us give chase."

"A moment, Doctor, for something tells me—" Mantis pointed to the shadows, his voice dropping. "*Quickly, we must hide ourselves!*"

Hopper leapt into a barrel,
drawing the lid over his head.
Through the plug-hole, he
had a view of the factory
yard. He scanned the
terrain for a sign of
Mantis, but the
inspector had melted
into the shadows, to wait,
for someone, or something.

Well, thought Hopper, I'm
comfortable enough, if sitting in an
inch of water is anyone's idea of comfort.

Hungry too. Racing about for hours like
this, with nothing in the old breadbasket.

But didn't I—

Let me see here, I think I—yes, I did!

From the watch pocket of his vest he
withdrew a small box of raisins, which he'd
completely forgotten in the heat of the chase.

Ah, what a godsend. Delicious, delicious . . .

Now if I just had a good book to read—

He leaned back in the barrel, trying to arrange his holding
position a bit, but something was sticking him between the
shoulder blades.

He reached behind and found, much to his surprise, a book,
wrapped in a waterproof bag and attached to the side of the
barrel.

Most peculiar. Book in a barrel, never heard of such a thing.

He held it up to the plug-hole, through which the moonlight was shining.

Illustrated History of Bugland, Volume II

Good heavens!

This is Gallgnat's work, to be sure.

I must tell Mantis at once.

The doctor attempted to straighten himself, but as he did so, a footstep sounded at the other end of the passage and he sank back down, to the bottom of the barrel.

The footsteps came nearer. He steeled himself for a struggle, but the footsteps moved slowly past the barrel, into the factory yard. There, in the dim light, he caught sight of their quarry. The figure turned, checking to make sure he was alone, and Hopper saw, not Gallgnat, but the even more unpleasant face of a hair-chewing chicken-louse.

The accomplice, thought Hopper. Come to pick up another coded message, which lies hidden in this barrel.

The chicken-louse, feeling certain he was unwatched, made for the barrel. He lifted the lid, put his hand down inside, and came up with Hopper's hat.

"Good evening," said Hopper, coming up after it.

The chicken-louse jumped back, into the arms of Mantis. "Thank you, Mr Chicken-louse, that will do." Mantis held the struggling enemy agent with an unbreakable grip.

"Who—who are you?"

"Servants, Mr Chicken-louse, of the Crown you sought to crumble."

The hair-chewing chicken-louse continued to struggle, as Mantis led him up the passageway. The *Illustrated History of*

Bugland, Volume II, was in the doctor's hands, and he noticed that under certain letters tiny pinholes had been made. By moving from letter to letter he began to read a message, quite different from the one intended by the author of the book. "I say, Mantis, I've found the coded part . . ."

"Yes," said Mantis, "and now we must find the chap who wrote it. But first—" He signaled for a cab that was passing on the lonely road. "—let us deposit this fine fellow with the authorities."

"You'll prove nothing," snarled their captive.

"We'll attempt to prove everything, Mr Chicken-louse," said Mantis, opening the carriage door and lifting the hair-chewing enemy agent up to the seat.

. . .

"Gallgnat will no doubt be in disguise." Mantis entered the railway waiting room, Hopper beside him, each of them carrying a piece of luggage, in the style of ordinary travelers.

"But how do you know it's a train he'll be taking?" asked Hopper.

"While we were trailing him to the factory, Doctor, I kept receiving the image of flashing trees, hills, houses—the view one would have from a racing train. He was obviously thinking about what his next step would be."

"Gad, Mantis, you have the most sensitive pair of feelers in Bugland."

"It is practice which has altered their scope, Doctor. You might do the same, if you were inclined to locate something other than a popcorn wagon."

"Here, now, Mantis, there's no need to be insulting."

"Only joking, Doctor, please forgive me." Mantis smiled. "You are an indispensable ally."

Hopper harumphed with embarrassment. And now, of course, it would be impossible to open the little zipper on his bag and have a handful of the emergency popcorn he'd packed in there, for Mantis would take the opportunity to chide him further.

"Seat yourself, Doctor, though I think our wait will be a brief one." Mantis dropped onto a bench, and tilted his head backward slightly, so that his delicate feelers were lifted at an angle. "There is a strong nervous excitement in the air, much greater than an ordinary passenger would create." He closed his eyes, and spoke softly, his voice almost a whisper now. "What I feel is the fear of a fleeing spy."

Then he seemed to sleep, as other of the waiting passengers on the benches were doing, and Hopper took the opportunity to quietly unzip his bag and take out a handful of the pink stuff.

Excellent. Still quite crisp . . .

The faintly audible munching sounds he made caused the trace of a smile to cross Mantis's lips. But devil take him, thought the doctor, I'm hungry.

However, before he had time for another handful of popcorn, his eyes were drawn to the door, where a tall, crouching figure had entered, weighed down by a large bag, his face almost completely masked by a scarf worn high on his neck.

Hopper turned to Mantis, who appeared to have fallen into the deepest sort of sleep.

Well, thought Hopper, I will simply bring this case to a conclusion myself, and won't Mantis be a little red-faced for having passed out on the job.

Hopper stood, and taking a stout grip on his cane, walked over to the tall, crouching passenger who had placed himself at the ticket window. Hopper got in behind the man and said quietly, "It's all up with you, Gallgnat. If you attempt to struggle I'll thrash you within an inch of your life."

The figure turned slowly. The scarf dropped slightly. The eye that riveted Doctor Hopper was cold, and the voice caustic. "Well, well—if it isn't Doctor *Pop*-corn."

The doctor stepped back, shocked. "Ah, excuse me, Baron Blowfly, I mistook you for—"

"For a *pop*-corn salesman?" The Baron fixed his scarf, purchased his ticket, and stalked away, leaving Doctor Hopper standing in confusion on the station floor.

But a shout from Mantis echoed behind him, and Hopper turned, in time to see the inspector moving after another figure, across the waiting room and out onto the platform.

Hopper took the room in two fast hops, and plunged through the station door. Mantis was already on the tracks, pursuing a tall, crouching gallgnat, whose cape floated on the air as he scrambled to the opposite platform.

"Halt!" cried Hopper, and joined the chase, over the gleaming rails. Mantis, in one leap, was on the inbound platform. The spy raced through the station doorway, and Mantis raced after him, diving at his bootheels and tripping him up. They

"Halt!" cried Hopper, and joined the chase.

tumbled together across the waiting-room floor, the spy drawing a jeweled dagger. He slashed at Mantis, who caught the thrust with his wrist, twisted the knife from Gallgnat's hand, and pinned him to the floor. "Cease struggling, Adrian Gallgnat, or I shall break all four of your arms."

Doctor Hopper closed in, along with the station policeman, and a crowd of passengers, who approached cautiously.

"Alright, now," said the policeman, "what's going on here?"

"I am Adrian C. Gallgnat," said Mantis's imprisoned prey, "attached to His Majesty's Embassy. And this ruffian—"

"I am Inspector Mantis, and this is the end of your game, Mr Gallgnat. Officer, there is overwhelming proof of espionage. I suggest you escort Mr Gallgnat to the nearest station house."

"Very good, Inspector," said the policeman. "Come along, you ..."

The struggling Gallgnat was led off, and Inspector Mantis straightened his cap. "I noticed you in conversation with Baron Blowfly, Doctor. Is he well?"

· · ·

Doctor Hopper sat by an early afternoon fire, working on his scrapbook, to which he now added the brief newspaper account of the capture of Adrian Gallgnat and his accomplice, the hair-chewing chicken-louse. At the other side of the room, Inspector Mantis was digging a dart out of the wall. A knock at the door caused them both to look up, and it was Hopper who opened it, while Mantis hid his darts behind his back.

"A letter for you, Doctor," said Mrs Inchworm, pressing it into the doctor's hand. "And such fancy stationery, too."

"Thank you, Mrs Inchworm, it was kind of you to bring

it . . ." The doctor gently closed the door against the landlady's curious gaze, and carried the letter over to his chair by the fire.

"Good news, Doctor?" asked Mantis, seeing the delighted expression on the doctor's face as he held the envelope up to the light, turning it this way and that.

"It's from the Duchess of Doodlebug," said Hopper brightly. "I wonder what could be in it?"

"Some people find opening a letter to be the solution to that problem," said Mantis, leaning over the edge of Hopper's chair.

"Aha! You're curious, Mantis, admit it! Admit that you're burning with curiosity and envious as the devil of what you know is in here—an invitation to call at the Doodlebug residence, for tea with Miss Laura Doodlebug."

"Are you expecting such a summons?"

"Why, of course! Just this Monday I sent my card around, suggesting I'd be free for the next several weekends."

"Then you have received the answer to your prayers," said Mantis, feigning a renewed interest in his darts, while Hopper tore open the envelope.

There was a long silence in the room, broken only by the crackling of the fire. When Mantis turned, it was to note that the envelope and its contents were in the fire, edges curling with smoke.

"I see it is a formal announcement, Doctor," said Mantis, as the flames licked through the engraved lettering.

"Indeed," said Hopper morosely.

"An announcement—of what?"

"Of the engagement of Laura Doodlebug to Baron Blowfly, that's what."

Mantis went to the cupboard and brought down a bag of small golden kernels, and the popper. "You'd better have some of this, old boy. You look rather done in."

"Thank you," said Hopper, accepting the popper. "Most kind of you."

"Don't mention it," said Mantis.

The two friends sat before the fire, watching the flames and listening to the bright popping sound of the popper, as a light afternoon rain began to fall outside, on Flea Street.

THE CASE OF
The Caterpillar's Head

Doctor Hopper stood at the stove, slowly stirring some fudge.

"You're going to be sick again," said Mantis, passing by him.

"Sick? Eh? Whatever can you mean, Mantis?"

"I mean," said Mantis, "sick from eating too much fudge."

Doctor Hopper poured the warm mixture into a waiting pan. "I'm perfectly capable of eating just *one* piece of fudge."

"The entire pan of it shall be gone in an hour, as you well know."

"See here, Mantis, I'm a medical practitioner. I should know what my constitution can endure in the way of fudge."

"Indeed," said Mantis, "you've eaten enough of it to publish a paper on the subject."

"Perhaps I will," said Hopper, contemplating the creamy sauce.

Mantis peered down at the pan. "It looks—frightfully good."

"Pity you won't be eating any," said Hopper.

"What if I were to offer—" Mantis gestured at the towering pile of pots and bowls the doctor had used. "—to do the dishes?"

"Then I might consider the matter."

The matter, however, was interrupted by a knock at the door.

"What's this?" said Mantis. "Have we another case?"

"I shouldn't doubt it," said the doctor. "But no power on earth shall come between me and these dozen pieces—" He began to slice squares in the thickened fudge.

Inspector Mantis opened the door. A slender young bug in blue stood on the threshold, delicate wings fluttering nervously. His eyes were enormous, and seemed to take in floor, ceiling, and all other parts of the room at once. "Is this the residence of Inspector Mantis?"

"It is," said Mantis. "Won't you come in?"

He led the slender bug to the arrangement of chairs at the fireplace, then stirred the smoldering log within it. The slender bug sat, and Doctor Hopper brought a plateful of cut fudge to the hearth bench. "Here we are, gentlemen. There is no case so pressing that it cannot be delayed a moment, for a mouthful of fudge."

Mantis reached for a piece. "I am forced to concur."

"Well," said the young bug, "I don't mind if I do," and in a few moments' time, the plate was empty.

Hopper smiled and went for more. This was the way a case should be conducted, with a continuous flow of the good things in life. He dished more fudge into the plate, and turned back, as Mantis leaned toward their visitor. "Your story, sir, would be most welcome, along with perhaps just one more plateful of—ah yes, Doctor, thank you, that is really most generous."

Another moment and the second plateful was empty. Hopper sat back, enjoying the warm sensation in his stomach. Their visitor, however, exhibited a restless tension, something obviously weighing heavily on his mind. "I am Rodney Damselfly," he said, toying nervously with the empty popcorn popper which rested beside him on the hearth.

Inspector Mantis straightened in his high-backed chair, his concentration suddenly so full and still, he seemed to have turned to stone. "You are good at tennis, Mr Damselfly, but careless with your money."

Damselfly sat up in his own chair, as if stuck with a pin. "How did you—"

"The way you are handling that popcorn popper is in the style of one striking at an invisible tennis ball." Mantis smiled. "That you are good at the game is something we might expect, from one whose eyes have 30,000 units, each capable of seeing the smallest part of an object in fine mosaic."

"It's true I play some tennis," said Damselfly, still toying with the popcorn popper. "But how did you know about the money I recently lost?"

"The edge of a pawn ticket protrudes from your pocket," said Mantis, stretching out his arm and plucking the ticket into the air, where he held it, tucked in his palm. "And what did you pawn? Easy to guess that, I think."

"Yes," said Damselfly sadly, "I pawned my racquet." He set the popper down and looked up at Mantis. "But that's just part of my bad luck. I've lost something much more valuable than that."

"Continue, Mr Damselfly. I'm most intrigued."

"I'm an easy-going fellow," said Damselfly, "as you may have suspected. And I've knocked about the world a bit. Well, quite recently, I bumped into a chap—met him on a ship, actually, where we struck up a conversation, talking of this and that—"

"The facts, Damselfly," said Mantis, with cold impatience.

"The fact is, he'd dug up a rare bit of treasure—the head of a caterpillar, preserved in amber. He said it was—" Damselfly leaned forward. "—one hundred million years old."

"A remarkable acquisition," said Mantis, putting a match to his pipe, a wreath of smoke quickly encircling his brow.

"Yes, it was remarkable," said Damselfly, "and beautiful too. I'd never seen anything so beautiful."

"Your acquaintance was planning to sell this unusual piece?"

"He was. And I was to help him find a buyer. As I said, I've been about a bit, and met many people, both high and low—"

Mantis shifted impatiently in his chair and Damselfly hurried on with his narrative. "—well, you see, he's disappeared.

Charlie Fungus-beetle has gone. Along with the hundred-million-year-old caterpillar's head."

"You suspect a crime?"

"His room has been ransacked."

Inspector Mantis unfolded his towering form from his high-backed chair. "I suggest you take us there, at once, Mr Damselfly."

Doctor Hopper rose from his own chair, hurried to the stove, and emptied the remaining fudge into his pocket.

• • •

The carriage wheels creaked beneath them, and Damselfly stared gloomily out the window. "I was to be given a small commission if I could find a buyer for the caterpillar's head. But now—"

"Now you must pawn your guitar."

Damselfly looked up, astonished. "How did you know about my guitar?"

"You are a man of few possessions, Damselfly. From the faint but obviously permanent creases on your fingertips, I deduce you play a stringed instrument. The guitar would suit you, I think, and that you should pawn it next is only logical."

The carriage began to slow, and Damselfly pointed out the window. "That's Charlie Fungus-beetle's place there. I hope you'll know as much about what happened to him as you know about me."

"We shall see," said Mantis, and a moment later Hopper, he, and Damselfly were entering a shabby rooming house. Damselfly led them through the hall and up the staircase. "Charlie's room is just ahead." Damselfly pointed. "The lock is broken. We can go right in."

Inspector Mantis entered, his eyes quickly sweeping the ransacked room. Doctor Hopper touched the edge of a worn, sagging chair. "Fungus-beetle's tastes were not extravagant."

"He was broke, same as me," said Damselfly. "But his luck, and mine, were changing, with that caterpillar head."

"Yes, most unfortunate that your piece of fortune should disappear." Mantis was going over every part of the small dark room with care, studying the opened drawers, the jumbled closet, the torn-up rug. "Well, what have we here?" he said, bending down beside Fungus-beetle's bed.

On the floor beside it were two little volcano-shaped cones, made of a fine, flaky substance, with a hole in the middle of each of them. Mantis touched the cones lightly, and they collapsed into dust. Out of the dust appeared a few nails, some metal eyelets, and a bit of thick thread. "These," said Mantis, "are all that remains of Fungus-beetle's shoes."

"That's Charlie Fungus-beetle's place . . ."

"His shoes!" exclaimed Doctor Hopper. "How extraordinary."

"Not altogether that extraordinary, Doctor." Mantis turned to Damselfly. "The ship you met Charlie Fungus-beetle on— did it sail out of Banana Land?"

Damselfly's enormous eyes became still more enormous. "Yes! Yes, it did!"

"As I thought," said Mantis, casting his gaze once more around the room.

"But how did you know?" begged Damselfly, following behind Mantis, toward the door, which Doctor Hopper was again opening.

"Be careful of that, Doctor," said Mantis. "It's about to—"

Even as he said it, the door was falling off in Hopper's hand, and a swirl of sawdust blew up at the doctor's feet. "Badly constructed," said Hopper, stepping over the fallen door.

"Sturdy enough," said Mantis, "until this morning. Isn't that right, Damselfly?"

"Yes," said Damselfly, "but how—"

"Tell me, Mr Damselfly, did you, as you'd hoped, find a buyer for the caterpillar's head?"

"I did," said Damselfly. "That was my good luck in this whole affair, for I happened to know a wealthy collector of antiquities. Met him on the tennis courts once. He has a shop on Weevil Street."

"Are you referring to Elliot Toadbug and Son, Ltd?"

"Yes, that's the man. Fungus-beetle and I were to meet with him this evening."

Mantis turned quickly toward the stairs. "We must leave you to your pawnbroker now, Mr Damselfly. In the meantime,

Doctor Hopper and I shall do our best with this case of the disappearing caterpillar's head."

"And Charlie Fungus-beetle," blurted Damselfly. "He's disappeared too."

"I regret to tell you," said Mantis slowly, "it is most unlikely you shall ever see Charlie Fungus-beetle again."

· · ·

"Well, Mantis, what do you make of it?" Doctor Hopper looked across the carriage at his companion, whose head nearly touched the roof.

"*Termes bellicosus*," said Mantis, chewing on his pipe.

"Eh?"

"Termites, my dear Hopper, Charlie Fungus-beetle fell in with a tribe of them. He pinched their sacred idol, the amber caterpillar's head. They followed him across the ocean, how we shall probably never know. But in any case, they found him."

"I see," said Hopper. "Termites would have eaten his door off the hinges . . ."

"And they ate his shoes as well. But what is more grotesque, they ate him."

"Good gracious!"

"Cannibals, Doctor. It is not a pretty thing. But Fungus-beetle knew the risk he was running. He gambled—" Mantis tapped his pipe out the window. "—and lost."

Doctor Hopper looked toward a bright row of shops up ahead. "We're approaching Weevil Street."

"And the shop of Toadbug and Son, Ltd. Driver!"

Mantis signaled and the carriage pulled over to the curb. Doctor Hopper stepped down, in front of Toadbug's window, where treasures from every age were displayed. There were vases, statues, lamps, but most impressive of all, perhaps, was an arrangement of jeweled flowers bearing the heavenly pistil of ovule, style, and stigma, each part rendered in rubies, diamonds, and emeralds of purest light. For a moment the jewels darkened, as a tall figure passed before the window, and then Mantis was through the door, Hopper behind him.

A younger Toadbug strode over in business-like fashion, but his projecting eyes were projected out farther than usual and were filled with anxiety. Mantis said coolly, "Then your father has disappeared?"

The younger Toadbug gave a start, jumping backwards before he could recover himself. "How did *you* know?" he asked suspiciously.

"My card," said Mantis, bending his tall form from the waist, toward the younger Toadbug.

"I see," said Toadbug Junior, his manner still not friendly. "Then you are investigating the case?"

"If you would tell us under what circumstances your father disappeared, we might be of assistance."

"He has gone," said Toadbug. "That is all I know."

"Had he, perchance, just come into possession of—a caterpillar's head, preserved in amber?"

Toadbug Junior went limp, and sagged into a dark, ornate chair, his anxiously projecting eyes projected at the floor. "Then you know everything."

"We know—something," said Mantis.

"He vanished last night, right after that Fungus-beetle fellow came round—"

"—with the caterpillar's head."

"How I wish I'd never seen the thing." Toadbug looked up, his round eyes filled with fear. "There was something about it that was haunted, as if a million faces were peering out of it toward me, their teeth grinding." Toadbug's hands went to his ears. "I hear it still! That horrible sound!"

"Munching on wood, Mr Toadbug, that's all it is. But you're fortunate they didn't eat your shop, and you. As for your father, we must act at once, if we are to save him." Mantis whirled about, his long coattails spinning with him, as he turned toward the magnificent display cases of Toadbug and Son. "Your father has been taken to a foreign land, by the powerful force of a secret army. To pursue them will take some financing—" Mantis bowed again, slightly. "—and I am a person of modest circumstances."

"Anything!" said the younger Toadbug, rising from his chair and gesturing round the room. "I have a fortune here . . ."

"A steamship ticket, for myself and my colleague, Doctor Hopper, will be sufficient."

"You have it," said Toadbug, reaching for his checkbook.

Mantis scribbled out a receipt. "We shall do everything in our power to rescue your father."

"Those million faces," said Toadbug, horror still written in his eyes.

"Tens of millions," said Mantis, calmly, and turning, made his way toward the door.

The waterboatmen were swinging cargo aboard, through clouds of fog that wrapped around the pilings and around the ship's black, gleaming hull. Mantis stepped onto the gangplank, carrying a small bag, and Hopper stepped after him, over the dark, lapping water.

"So," said Hopper as they climbed the gangplank, "Fungus-beetle sold the caterpillar's head to Toadbug and Son without cutting Damselfly in."

"Chaps like Fungus-beetle know no honor," said Mantis. "And Damselfly would have done the same, no doubt, if roles

had been reversed. It's just unfortunate that the elder Toadbug should have been drawn into the scheme. After all, he didn't know he was buying a sacred idol."

"Do you think we have a chance to save him?"

"I do."

"But why should the termites spare him?"

"For ransom. Or for other reasons, less likely to please old man Toadbug, I'm sure."

"Torture?"

"Perhaps. Or a public execution. After all—" Mantis turned at the ship's rail, and bent his elbows upon it, facing toward the fog-shrouded city. "—he bought their sacred caterpillar as if it were no more than a pretty stickpin. They must stand in awe of that, enough to warrant carrying him back to the King and Queen of Banana Land."

Doctor Hopper set his bag down. "How far off it seems at this moment—"

The ship's horn sounded, the waterboatmen gathered in the anchor ropes, and the great ship moved, away from the pier, toward the sea.

· · ·

Mantis sat in his deck chair, a book open on his lap, a sparkling ocean beyond him. "Listen to this, Doctor, from my little guide-book to Banana Land: *They will eat your trunk, your coat and hat. They will even eat your wooden leg, should you have one, turning it into a heap of sawdust by morning.*'"

"Charming place," said Hopper. This entire affair, certain to be drawn out for some time, would mean he'd miss the Cricket

Match next week. His favorite players would be participating, and he'd be in Banana Land, with someone trying to eat his hat.

· · ·

"Ah," said Mantis, standing at the bow, "there it is, Doctor, with its million mysteries awaiting us. What greater game is there than this?"

"A Cricket Match," said Hopper, looking at his watch. "Just about to start."

"Oh come now, old fellow, surely you don't want to be a spectator all the time."

"I enjoy being a spectator," said Hopper. "I like the quiet, comfy life, Mantis. I'm not a mad devil like you."

The breeze from Banana Land blew the first fragrance to them, then, as the ship's bow cut through the coastal waters. Mantis leaned forward, inhaling deeply. "Amongst these many tangled scents is the trace of Elliot Toadbug, whom we shall find, by heaven." Mantis brought his fist down softly on the ship's rail, as the ship's horn blew, announcing their entrance to the harbor.

· · ·

"I'll guide you to the termites," said the grizzled old mining beetle. "But it won't be an easy trip, nor a safe one." He looked across the table of the jungle café, toward Mantis and Hopper, then pointed to the jungle wall. "There's everything out there —terrible species you've only seen in your nightmares." The mining beetle wiped his nose with his sleeve and took another sip of orchid nectar, drops of it spilling into his filthy whiskers. He gasped, sputtered, and set the drink back down, an evil grin on his face. "Do you understand what I'm saying, sirs?"

"I think so, Mr Beetle—"

"*Suck*beetle," said the miner, frowning at them, and then puffing himself up. "J. *P*. Suckbeetle, if you don't mind."

"Very well, Mr Suckbeetle," said Mantis, standing, "since we understand each other, I suggest we leave at once."

"In a hurry to die?" The old miner laughed. "Well, alright then!" He struggled to his feet and they followed him out of the café, into the street of the tropical city. Beside it were the dark arms of the giant jungle trees, serpents wrapped around them, their eyes glittering in the sunlight. J. P. Suckbeetle spat at them drunkenly, and weaved forward, through the mud.

"Gad, Mantis," said Hopper in a low whisper, "you've chosen a ruined wretch to lead us through—*that*?" He gestured toward the deadly jungle.

"I should think you and I would both be mad as J. P. Suckbeetle if we'd stayed out here our whole lives long." Mantis's long arms swung languidly at his sides. "But we'd also know where the termites are."

"Yes," growled Suckbeetle, turning toward them. "The Lost City of the Termites, gentlemen, a sight you shall never forget."

. . .

The campfire flickered, casting ominous shadows on the faces of the three gathered around it. J. P. Suckbeetle spat into the fire. "I've seen it all." He stared at the dancing flames. "I've seen their secret rituals. I've lived in their city."

Doctor Hopper shook his campcan full of popping popcorn. "How did you manage that?"

"They tolerated me. I did them little favors. I was *handy* to have around." J. P. Suckbeetle lifted his head, his beady eyes gleaming in the firelight. "I was just one of many who'd penetrated the city. There were others. Termite-lovers, they call us."

"I detect no love in your voice, Mr Suckbeetle," said Mantis.

"I loved the splendor of it." Suckbeetle looked up from the fire, toward the jungle night. "I love the inner chambers of the palace. You could wander there forever and never come to the end."

"Have you ever seen the caterpillar's head? "

"I saw it, plenty of times, up there on the altar. They worshipped it, along with their King and Queen."

"And Charlie Fungus-beetle stole it."

J. P. Suckbeetle looked up. "You know Charlie, do you?"

"We know the remains of his shoes," said Mantis. "The pleasure of meeting Charlie was denied us."

"A good sort," said Suckbeetle. "Reckless though. Bound to run into trouble with them termites sooner or later."

"Sooner, I think, than he expected," said Mantis, elbows propped on his bony knees, his pipe smoldering under his chin.

. . .

J. P. Suckbeetle parted a last curtain in the jungle wall, and pointed to a great grey pagoda in the center of an enormous plain. "Look at it, the cursed place! And yet I love it, and find myself returnin' to it, always . . ."

"If you'd spare us your poetic sentiments, Mr Suckbeetle," said Mantis, "we'd be most grateful."

Doctor Hopper gazed at the military guard surrounding the palace, their bright helmets passing back and forth in front of the many gates. "How shall we get past them?"

"We must wait until nightfall," said Suckbeetle.

"We must enter—*now*," said Mantis.

"Oh, we must, must we? And do you suppose you're invisible, Mr Mantis? You're big as a stick, you are. You'll have those soldiers all over us in a second. No, we must wait until night-fall."

"A stick, did you say, Mr Suckbeetle?" Mantis stepped forward, toward some high green blades of razor grass, where he froze, like a blade of the grass itself. A moment more and he had faded altogether from view.

"Well, that's clever enough," said Suckbeetle, and closed the emerald green curtain back across his and Doctor Hopper's hideout in the leaves.

. . .

As night fell, Doctor Hopper followed Suckbeetle out of the leaves, onto the vast moonlit plain. Soldier guards were stationed everywhere, but J. P. Suckbeetle was able to find his way on by them. "*I know these parts*," he rasped. "*I know my way around.*"

Doctor Hopper kept low, not trusting Suckbeetle for a moment, but absolutely dependent on him now. Helmeted soldiers were tramping the grass only a few paces away, their weapons shining in the moonlight.

I could be home listening to the tender kernels popping in the fire, thought Doctor Hopper. Instead I'm charging through the bush behind a half-mad old miner. Confound Mantis! And the devil take Elliot Toadbug and Son, Ltd!

Hopper's mustaches twitched, and J. P. Suckbeetle rushed them forward, past a parading patrol of soldiers. A clicking sound filled the air, and Hopper saw sharp points of armor on the soldiers' legs brushing back and forth, producing the sound. At two clicks, they turned on their flank and Suckbeetle, anticipating the signal, scuttled on by them, Hopper close behind, holding his hat.

Hopper's antennae twitched. He received a bright green image, from Mantis, somewhere near—a signal that the soldiers couldn't detect. But their footsteps seemed to say—*our enemy is always around us.*

Suckbeetle scuttled up a few more paces, until the grey steps of the palace were at hand. He pointed at an opening in the side of the palace wall. *"Now,"* he growled, and slipped through the chamber opening, followed by Hopper, just as the soldiers turned on their heels, heading back.

But Hopper and Suckbeetle were already making their way through the inner chamber, where workers came and went, rushing about on palace errands.

"We're alright now," said J. P. Suckbeetle confidently. "Once you're inside, they won't bother you." He chuckled, looking at Hopper. "Well, at least they won't bother *me.*"

"And what," whispered Hopper, "is so special about you?"

"They like my filthy whiskers," laughed Suckbeetle. He stuck out his grizzled chin. "My beard always has some kind of juice spilling into it and the workers like to suck it. That's why—"

"—you are called Suckbeetle. But what about me?"

"We'll soon find out," chuckled Suckbeetle, pointing at a group of workers coming toward them.

Doctor Hopper leapt into the shadows of another hall, deciding that he had to take his own chances now, but he peeked back around the corner when he heard Suckbeetle laughing again.

"Har, har, har . . ."

The lady workers had gathered around the miner, and were licking at his nectar-soaked whiskers, their abdominal segments clicking excitedly.

Hopper opened his pocket and took out a piece of homemade fudge. He applied it to his mustache ends, like wax, turning the ends upward.

Then he moved further on down the dark hall. The clicking language of the termites sounded all around him. The entire palace echoed with it, signals passing everywhere.

He glided, and listened, then glided again, along the inner way of the palace. The chambers were a labyrinth, housing millions, with a great commotion everywhere, ever larger gatherings of workers appearing at each corner. Owing to the growing crowds, he was able to move more freely, as if through the marketplace of a city street. Other strangers were in the crowd, mostly drunken beetles, laughing it up.

"Oh," said a soft voice, *"how sweet you smell."*

Hopper turned toward the voice, but all he heard was the clicking noise again, from the abdominal section of a worker, who was making her way straight for him.

"I say, miss—" Hopper stepped back, but the young lady

had already licked the fudge off his mustache ends, her dark polished mouth opening and closing with frightening speed.

"*More—*" said the soft voice, before it was covered by clicking noises again.

"I must be off," said Hopper, lifting his hat. "I have an engagement—to see the Queen."

He hurried away, losing himself in the crowd again. Beetle traders moved there, carousing and shouting, and soldiers worked their way through, patrolling for less welcome intruders, their clicking armor saying once more—*our enemy is everywhere.*

Their swords and helmets flashed, and moved on, leaving Doctor Hopper to cross the crawling avenue, to the next chamber, where a huge vaulted garden appeared, the walls of it covered with rows of hanging fungus. Termite farmers were tending it, fertilizing it with bits of decaying wood, and gathering the liquid secretion that dripped from it. Doctor Hopper snuck into the garden, and tip-toed beneath the hanging vines. Then, noticing a drop of liquid dripping above his head, he could not resist, and stuck out his tongue to catch it.

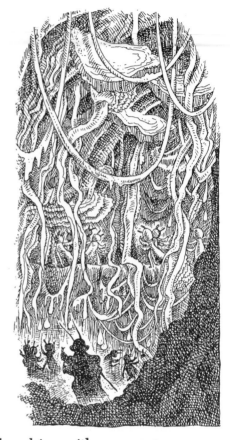

Pungent, but good. Yes, it would go nicely with popcorn, pour it on like melted butter . . .

His antennae suddenly curled, pulsing with a message.

Hopper! This is no time for culinary considerations!

"*Mantis!*" said Hopper in a whisper. "*Where are you?*"

But the line was dead, and the only sound was the clicking of the farmers as they hung more fungus from the ceiling. Hopper hurried on, out of the great garden, toward the next chamber, and the next. He knew now that he might very well wander in the colony for the rest of his life, and never find the way back out, for every chamber was the same, and there were countless numbers of them. He tapped his derby with his cane, and pressed onward, humming to himself, *There'll always be a Bugland somewhere, a little bit of Bugland in the air.*

The clicks, though confusing, were getting louder. He followed them, and the clicking soon became a single powerful droning noise, the halls vibrating with it. He felt his way along, holding the walls, feeling the vibration getting stronger, then turned a corner and saw the army guard, placed in front of what must surely be the central chamber of the colony.

It was again time to use the subterfuge learned from J. P. Suckbeetle. He had one last little piece of fudge left. He touched up his mustache ends with it and stepped forward into the hall.

The soldiers spun toward him, their swords raised, their armor glistening, and their clicking a sharp command to halt.

"I'm the Ambassador from Bugland," said Hopper. "I have an appointment with your Queen." The doctor displayed his sweet mustache ends prominently, and the soldiers stepped aside, allowing his audacious entrance to be made, into the central chamber.

The sight he beheld was staggering.

The chamber was a teeming mass of workers and slaves, attending to their Queen, who reigned from a great dais. And on the throne beside her, a crown on his head, was none other than Elliot Toadbug, Ltd!

Then Hopper saw the old termite King, laid out on a funeral bier, his arms folded on his chest.

Had Toadbug murdered him?

No, the King looked old, and dried-out. Hopper saw that the King was actually a mummy, long-dead. In his place was Elliot Toadbug and hanging over Toadbug, high up on the wall, was the sacred piece of amber, with the ancient caterpillar's head preserved inside it.

Hopper stared at it, entranced, until a minister of the Queen came forward, soldiers on both sides of him, and pointed at Doctor Hopper's mustache.

"Here, now," said Hopper, "take your hands off me." But the soldiers were already dragging him toward the Queen. Doctor Hopper removed his derby. "Your Majesty, I am the Ambassador from Bugland."

He bowed before her. But as he did so, old man Toadbug laughed.

"The Ambassador from Bugland? Don't hand us that!" He snapped his fingers and the soldiers grabbed Hopper once more. "Take him to the dungeons," snarled Toadbug the King, Ltd.

"Why," cried Doctor Hopper, "I came to save you!"

"Well, then," remarked Toadbug, "you shall have no trouble saving yourself."

"But first," said a queenly voice, *"let me lick his mustache ends."*

The soldiers shoved Doctor Hopper closer to the barbarous Queen. Her metallic mouth moved with lightning speed, and the remaining fudge was gone from Doctor Hopper's mustache.

The Queen smiled, and spoke, but it was once again only clicking that Hopper heard, as the soldiers dragged him away.

The doctor struggled, his eyes still riveted on the smug figure of Elliot Toadbug, seated on the throne.

"Toadbug!" he shouted. "You'll pay for this!"

"Toadbug always pays," said Toadbug, laughing.

. . .

Doctor Hopper hung in chains, deep in a subterranean chamber. Other prisoners hung there too, none of them living, the life long ago having been drained from them, their bodies no more than glittering shells.

"A foul place," said Hopper to himself, his derby hanging in his eyes and his foot itching where he couldn't scratch it.

Then, a green light flashed, and his antennae quivered.

Hopper watched from under the brim of his derby, toward the dungeon doorway, where two guards were posted. They were clicking together, their voices laughing, apparently one telling a joke to the other.

But the joke, unfortunately, was on them. A long green arm moved out, throttling both, and they fell limp on the dungeon floor as the shadow of Mantis appeared, enormous in the doorway.

"Mantis!" called Hopper from his dark corner. "Here I am!"

Mantis stepped through, followed by a number of small loutish-looking grubs. "Temporarily allied to us, Doctor," said Mantis, undoing the doctor's chains. "They know the palace, and have agreed to lead us through, provided you give them your remaining fudge."

"But I smeared the last of it in my mustache."

"Your emergency ration, Doctor. Have you forgotten it?"

"Why—right you are!" Hopper quickly removed his derby and took a handful of candycorn from the lining, which he distributed to the rough-and-tumble grubs.

"Who are these fellows, Mantis? What's their stake in the game?"

"They eke a small living out here in the palace, begging, borrowing, scavenging around. They'll do anything for sweets, as you can see." Mantis nodded toward the grubs, who were devouring Hopper's offering. "They're simple chaps, Doctor, I suggest you pretend that your derby is a never-ending store of candycorn."

Hopper made a few more passes with his derby, as suggested, and the grubs punched each other for the meager rewards issuing from it; then the procession moved on, up out of the dark underground chamber.

"Did you know," said Hopper, "that Toadbug has usurped the throne?"

"Fever, Doctor," said Mantis, moving into an upper hallway with long, silent strides. "Elliot Toadbug is more than a little out of his mind at the moment."

"He seemed uncommonly lucid when he ordered me into chains."

"Indeed a thoughtless gesture," said Mantis, "but he cannot be held altogether responsible for his actions. The ants have altered his mental state."

"You mean—he's drugged?"

"He's been eating nothing but fungus since he arrived," said Mantis. "He's completely forgotten that he's a shopkeeper from Bugland. He believes he's always been here, reigning in the palace."

"But why have they accepted him?" asked Hopper, fending off a grub who was trying to grab his derby for more candy-corn.

"Because of the caterpillar's head. The soldiers brought him back with it, and that was enough for the Queen."

"But can't she see that Toadbug is just—" Doctor Hopper grew red in the face with exasperation. "—just a toadbug!"

The grubs interrupted all talk, with a signal that an important turn was ahead, one which led, Doctor Hopper saw, to the rear entrance of the throne, a place free from soldiers. Only workers were seen, going in and out, attending to the King and Queen's wishes.

"*Observe,*" said Mantis in a whisper, indicating a crack in the mortared wall. Doctor Hopper peered through, and saw a worker bringing a bowl of fungus soup to Toadbug, who drank it back with a wild laugh, his projecting eyes projected quite out of his head, dizzy with the dreamlike spectacle before him —of thousands, millions, looking up to him for favor. Among them, Hopper saw a familiar grizzled face. "There's J. P. Suckbeetle."

"Suckbeetle has his part to play . . ." Mantis edged toward the rear doorway of the throne. His long green arm extended out, looking like the slender stem of a royal umbrella plant, only one among many held over the King and Queen's head. With his other arm, Mantis fished in his tobacco pocket and brought out a match, which he struck, allowing the signal flame to burn momentarily in the air.

As it flashed, the voice of J. P. Suckbeetle bellowed out from below the dais. "Try *my* whiskers, your Highness! You remember me, don't you? From the old days? Har, har, har!" The drunken miner climbed toward the throne. The Queen, seeing the old bum, flushed with anger, but then, as Suckbeetle neared, her eyes seemed to blink with recognition, and her manner grew more gentle.

"*Come here,*" the soft clicks seemed to say, and Suckbeetle swaggered toward her.

"Just for you, yer Highness," he said, fluffing out his tangled, dripping whiskers.

Mantis murmured, almost to himself. "The strange mystery of a Queen's past . . ."

Doctor Hopper stared through his own crack. "She . . . she seems to like the old fool."

Mantis sighed. "Such is fate, Doctor. J. P. Suckbeetle's whiskers were the sweetest she'd ever known."

The drunken miner climbed toward the throne.

As Suckbeetle gave an intoxicated bow before the Queen, Elliot Toadbug was momentarily forgotten by the palace guard. A long green stem separated from the umbrella plant, wrapped itself around Toadbug's throat and lifted him into the air. Toadbug's eyes bulged still further out, but his cry was held silent in Mantis's devastating grip.

The inspector deposited him in the back hall, among the grubs. "Mr Toadbug, we are taking you home."

"This is my home!" snarled Toadbug, pointing toward the seething crowd of workers, soldiers, slaves, and parasites that filled the throne room.

"No, Mr Toadbug, it is not. Your home is back on Weevil Street, and that, old chap, is where you're going now." Mantis and Hopper each held an arm, and the grubs led the way, through the labyrinthine halls.

The twisting, turning journey was swift, with only brief stops, demanded by the grubs, during which Doctor Hopper threw more candycorn at them, from his derby. "I'm running desperately low, Mantis. Are we anywhere near the exit?"

"It can't be far, Doctor, for I hear noises from the courtyard."

The grubs, hearing the noises too, suddenly stopped, listened again, and then vanished in a frightened rush.

"What does this mean?" asked Hopper, as the sound grew louder.

"I believe," said Mantis, "the colony is at war."

The sound of thousands of clanking swords penetrated the walls, and a moment later the halls were filled with palace guards, rushing to defend the courtyard.

Hopper and Mantis pressed back into the shadows of the hall. Toadbug was mumbling, lost in a dream, his eyes unfocussed, his head bowed. "...yes, your Majesty... certainly, your Majesty..."

"Steady on there," said Mantis softly, holding Toadbug up.

"Off with their heads," muttered Toadbug, staggering along.

As they turned the next corner, Mantis directed Hopper's attention to an opening above them in the palace wall.

"What is it?" asked Hopper.

"An air duct," said Mantis. "The palace is ventilated and cooled by a vast network of them. It is through them I first entered, and it is by them we shall leave." He put out his slender arm and lifted Doctor Hopper up to the duct, then turned to Toadbug. "Now then, Mr Toadbug, up you go..."

"... let them eat cake ..." Toadbug was lifted up, into the air duct. "... let them ... eat ..."

Mantis crawled up last, then struck out behind him, collapsing dirt and debris into the opening of the duct, so that none might follow them.

"*Mantis,*" called Hopper from up ahead in the duct, "*where am I going?*"

"Straight ahead, Doctor. All the vents finally lead to the outer wall."

". . . long live the King . . . long live . . ." Toadbug's eyes were wobbling around in his head, strange hallucinations still tormenting the shopkeeper as he crawled. ". . . the riches . . . the wonders . . . they're mine . . . all mine . . ."

Hopper felt ahead of him in the dust, and suddenly, before he could stop, he was hanging off the side of the palace wall.

Warm jungle breezes blew over him for a moment, and then Mantis snatched him back up, into the duct.

"Thank you, old man," said Hopper, "I was almost a goner." He adjusted his derby and secured himself just at the edge of the duct, with Mantis and Toadbug beside him, looking down at the spectacle of war taking place beneath them in the courtyard, where countless swords clashed and clanged. The forces

of another colony were besieging the palace gates, and the home soldiers were defending it with all their might. Nonetheless, the enemy had penetrated the palace in many places, and prisoners were being taken.

"We must sue for peace," mumbled Toadbug.

"We must find J. P. Suckbeetle." Mantis drew out a length of strong silken line, which he fastened to a root imbedded in the air duct. The other end he hung free, down the palace wall. "Doctor, down you go—and now you, Mr Toadbug . . ."

". . . the King was in the countinghouse . . ."

"That's right, Mr Toadbug, counting up his money. Hang on and drop slowly . . ." Mantis came on the line after Toadbug and the three shadows descended the palace wall and then dropped into the courtyard below.

"*Suckbeetle,*" hissed Mantis into the darkness. "*Are you there.*"

A coarse laugh came in answer, and then Suckbeetle swaggered out of the bushes, accompanied by two ladies of the palace, who were affectionately stroking his whiskers, and then licking their fingers. "I've got to leave you now, girls," said Suckbeetle, "but I'll be back. J. P. Suckbeetle will return."

"If you're quite through with your farewells, Mr Suckbeetle," said Mantis, "might I remind you we are surrounded by an army?"

"Stick with Suckbeetle," said the old miner, and crouched low, disappearing back into the bushes, with Mantis, Hopper, and Toadbug following, through a courtyard ringing with battle.

Toadbug collapsed, and called for more soup. Mantis swung him over one shoulder and proceeded. Toadbug's bewildered eyes were staring toward the ground. ". . . where . . . where am I?"

Soldiers raced past them, the uniforms of both colonies show-

ing in the moonlight, and sharp clicking orders were shouted everywhere, but Suckbeetle anticipated each move they made, and snuck his party past them, across the plain.

"Admirable work, Suckbeetle," said Mantis, as they entered the deep curtain of the jungle.

"I know my way around," said the swaying miner. "Ask anyone you meet in this land about J. P. Suekbeetle." The miner opened his shirt and took out a flask of spiritous nectar, which he swigged down, spilling most of it in his beard. "They'll tell you I know every inch of this cursed place—"

"I'm sure character references abound, Mr Suckbeetle."

Mantis turned to Toadbug, who was staring back at the palace, his face a puzzled frown. Mantis touched the shopkeeper gently on the shoulder. "Say goodbye to your fantastic kingdom, Mr Toadbug, for you are homeward bound."

"A . . . dream," stammered Toadbug. "I've had . . . an incredible dream."

"Quite so," said Mantis. Then, steadying Toadbug, he turned, and they followed J. P. Suckbeetle, along the secret jungle path.

· · ·

"Home," said Toadbug, as the carriage rolled up Weevil Street. "I can hardly believe I'm here." The elder Toadbug stared out the window at the familiar facade of the street, and sighed when he saw his own shop, with *Toadbug and Son, Ltd* curving in bright gold letters above the door.

The carriage creaked to a stop, and Toadbug stepped down. "Gentlemen, I owe you my life. Come into my shop. Take anything you find there, with my compliments."

"The adventure is its own reward," said Mantis, settling back in his carriage seat. But Toadbug remained motionless in the doorway, an air of bewilderment suddenly clinging to him again. Mantis spoke gently at the window. "Go in, Mr Toadbug. Your son is waiting for you."

"How . . . how shall I be able to take up my business, after all I have known?" He looked pleadingly at Mantis and Hopper, as if asking that they carry him back to the monstrous beauty of the jungle; but finally he turned, and extended a reluctant hand to the door. The little bell above the door sounded with a tinkling ring, and Mr Toadbug's soul seemed to answer. He smiled, touched the little bell fondly, and entered the shop.

Mantis signaled to the driver of the carriage, and it rolled on, up Weevil Street. "Well, Doctor, things did not turn out too badly in the end. And you were kissed by the Queen."

"Not an honor I'd care to have repeated," said Hopper, stroking his mustache ends. As he did so, a faint clicking noise went off in his ear drums, and then echoed, ever more faintly, down and down through his nerves. "I say—"

"The Queen's signal," said Mantis. "Once heard, it is never forgotten."

Hopper looked out the window, fearful for a moment that they were being followed, even as Charlie Fungus-beetle had been followed, across the sea. But as he gazed at the wet brick streets, and at the reflection of his calm, silent companion in the window, he knew the Case of the Caterpillar's Head was indeed finished, forever.

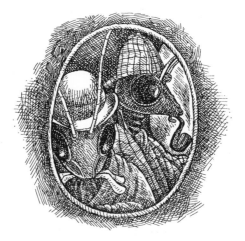

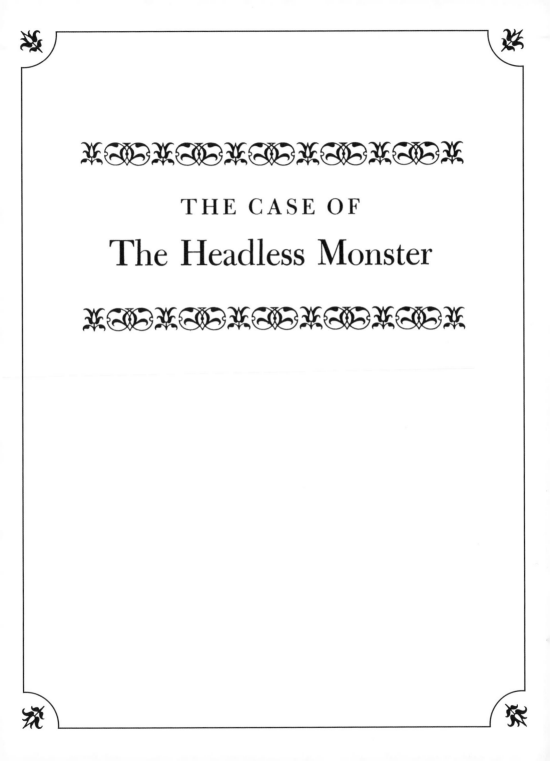

THE CASE OF
The Headless Monster

IT WAS ONCE AGAIN that time of year when Doctor Hopper concocted his famous blackberry pie. The little flat on Flea Street was a jumble of pots, pans, rolling pins and bowls, everything lightly dusted with flour, including Hopper himself, whose jacket and pants were nearly snow-white.

He was bent over, checking the oven door, for his famous pie (famous only to himself) was now baking within. "It looks frightfully good, Mantis."

Around the corner in the sitting room, Inspector Mantis was seated at his desk, a large volume open before him, on the subject of fossil-forms. The inspector's attention was riveted, however, not upon the book, but upon a tower he was in the process of constructing out of some dice, a pencil, a pen knife and several erasers, all balanced one atop the other. "*I almost have it, Hopper,*" he said under his breath, as he carefully laid a single paperclip on the topmost point.

"I believe it's done," answered Hopper, and opened the oven door. The crust let forth a divine aroma, and the doctor, clutching a pair of flowered pot-holders, brought the pie forth. "A triumph . . ." He carried the steamy, bubbling creation to the sideboard.

". . . just one more . . . story . . ." Mantis had an ornate little pollen box in his fingertips, from which he sometimes took a pinch; at the moment he was lowering it slowly and carefully onto the top of his precariously balanced tower. The pollen box was jeweled—a present from the King of Ailanthus at the successful conclusion of the case of the Petrified Water Prince. Mantis lowered the little box onto the pinnacle, where it rested perfectly, until a knock came at the door, causing Mantis's bony knee to jump, strike the desk, and send the tower toppling.

He quickly gathered the fallen pieces, closed the desk, and made his way to the door. A springtail bug stood on the threshold, nervously curling his tail beneath him in a tightened coil. "Is this the residence of Inspector Mantis?"

"It is," said Mantis. "Won't you please come in?"

The springtail entered, by the curious mechanism of releasing his coiled tail and springing forward. Doctor Hopper, unaware of a visitor, came out in his apron (borrowed from Mrs Inchworm and trimmed with lace), just as the springtail landed. The springtail looked up at the apron. "*You*," he asked, "are the famous Doctor Hopper?"

"Why . . . yes," stammered Hopper, attempting to tuck up the lacy edges of the apron. "So I am."

Mantis intervened. "Doctor Hopper is in the midst of a delicate experiment—"

"Smells like pie," said the springtail.

"And so it is," said Hopper. "Look here, gentlemen, I see no reason why we shouldn't all sit down to a hot, steaming slice of—"

"Trouble," said the springtail, "Very bad trouble."

"Trouble?" asked Mantis.

"—blackberry pie," said Hopper,
trying to save the situation, but
Mantis was already directing the
springtail toward a chair, and Hopper
saw that neither of them was interested
in his juicy, flaky, bubbling creation. Well,
so be it, he said to himself. More's the pie
for me. And he returned to his sideboard.

But once there, he could not help over-
hearing the conversation in the sitting room.

". . . terrible apparition . . . frightening all residents . . ."

The springtail went on, describing some sort of menacing
form which had been haunting the neighborhood of Fungus
Four Corners. ". . . appears to be *headless* . . ."

Headless, thought Doctor Hopper. What utter nonsense.

He cut a piece of pie and laid it on a plate.

There, that should make a satisfactory beginning. Now . . .

". . . we thought that you, Inspector Mantis, might be per-
suaded to come to Fungus Four Corners . . ."

Doctor Hopper contemplated the hot steaming slice, too hot
at the moment, but soon to cool, and then bring joy in equal
measure to the long labor he had expended in its preparation.
He was good with apple, and half-decent with peach, but
blackberry was his speciality. He lifted his fork and toyed with
the edge of the crust, half-listening as the springtail went on
in the other room.

". . . pay all expenses, of course, and consider it our greatest good fortune if you would investigate this monstrous form that has so terrorized our quiet countryside . . ."

Hopper buried his fork through the crust and into the heart of the pie. Lovingly he lifted a sizable piece into the air and savored its aroma.

The moment, he said to himself as he brought the fork toward his mouth, has come.

"Hopper," called Mantis, "the chase is on!" The inspector came round the kitchen door and clutched Hopper by the shoulder. "Hurry, old boy, we've no time to lose."

The forkful of pie fell back to the plate. "Mantis, have you no shred of decency in you? I was about to take my first taste!"

"Your pie must wait, Doctor. We have work ahead of us."

"Wait? It can't wait. In an hour it will be cold."

"In an hour this case may have changed round again, and gotten beyond our grasp. Come, Doctor . . ." Mantis lifted his companion by the elbow and dragged him toward the coat rack.

"Fiend!" shouted Hopper as his derby was plopped on his head. "Blackguard!" he cried, as Mantis dropped a coat around him and rushed him toward the door, where the springtail was waiting, his tail bent anxiously beneath him.

"Now, Mr Springtail," said Mantis to their client, "we are ready."

"I apologize," said Springtail to Hopper, "for this interruption."

". . . fiddlesticks . . ." muttered Hopper, trailing down the stairs behind the springing Springtail and the loping Mantis, who moved ahead of him, into the fog-bound street.

. . .

The train rattled along over the rails, past cottages, farms, and country estates. "Exactly how many times," asked Mantis, "has this apparition been seen?"

"Countless times of late," said Springtail, "so often that we do not let our children out even by day, and none of us, unless armed, venture out at all after dark."

"Has anyone ever gotten close to the thing?" asked Hopper, his manner somewhat calmer now, his famous pie receding ever further into the background, with each toot of the train's whistle.

"I've been close enough to it never to want to be so close again," said Springtail.

"And what exactly does it look like?" asked Mantis.

"Ghastly. Hideous. The most nightmarish—"

"A precise anatomical description would be more helpful, Mr Springtail," said Mantis, somewhat impatiently, but then excused himself. "Forgive me, I forget that you have suffered a severe shock, but our inquiry must proceed on as factual a basis as possible."

"Well, it *was* headless," said Springtail. "Of that I'm certain."

"How so?"

"There were no eyes, no mandibles, no maxillae, tooth, nor tongue." Springtail shivered all over. "There was only a headless body, moving toward me, feeling its way along."

"Were you threatened by it?"

Springtail wiped his brow. "My sanity was threatened, that I can assure you, and I've taken my place as one of those who has seen the grim gruesome thing and can no longer sleep at night." Springtail again wiped his brow, as if to wipe the memory of the headless monster away. "I used to be an athletic sort, Inspector, competing in the amateur high jumps, and hurdles, and such, but the spring has gone right out of me. I hardly even bounce these days . . ."

The conductor of the train appeared in the doorway of the coach. "Fungus Four Corners, next. Fungus Four Corners will be next . . ."

"Well," said Mantis, rising cheerfully from his seat, "we shall soon have our own chance to see your monster."

"You shall not find it a pleasant encounter," said Springtail, taken aback by the smile on Mantis's face.

Hopper, perceiving Springtail's discomfort, apologized for his companion. "Mantis is a connoisseur of the unusual. The more bloodcurdling a situation, the more enjoyment he seems to take from it."

"Well," said Springtail, springing down onto the station platform, "he will have a taste he won't forget, this time."

. . .

"The ancestral home." Springtail gestured out the carriage

"*Exactly how many times has this apparition been seen?*"

window to a sweeping panorama of sea and sky, the center of which was a large old mansion, built on a rugged cliffside.

"A noble dwelling," said Mantis, gazing at its high roofs and balconies.

"My uncle awaits you," said Springtail, as the carriage stopped, and Mantis saw a white-haired old soldier coming out onto the great porch of the house.

"He is—?"

"Colonel Bristletail, of the Highland Pinchers, now retired." Springtail opened the carriage door and sprang down. "But you'll find him still full of powder and shot."

The old colonel descended the steps and extended his hand. "Mantis, eh? I've heard of you. You assisted a friend of mine."

"I'm afraid I don't recall—"

"Does the name Blister Beetle ring a bell? Chap in the potato business?"

Mantis smiled. "The Rotten Wood Affair."

"Handled to everyone's satisfaction," said the Colonel. "Blister Beetle still mutters about it occasionally." The harsh old trooper adjusted his steel-rimmed monocle. "We expect no less of you in this matter."

"You have seen the monster?"

"The loathsome thing came at me during my evening stroll." Colonel Bristletail again adjusted his monocle, which seemed to be in the habit of popping out. "I've faced a thousand charging army ants, sir, and never flinched a muscle, but this thing turned me white, right down to my spurs."

"Have you any idea what attracted the creature to you, Colonel?"

"None. As I say, I was on my evening stroll and was quite plunged in my thoughts. I'm preparing a memoir of the Army Ant Wars, you see." The colonel pointed with his monocle, toward the forest. "We still get the occasional uprising to the south, but of course it's nothing like the great campaigns in which I served when I was young . . ."

Mantis stared across the grounds to the southern forest. "It was not, perhaps, an army ant you saw?"

"You think I don't know what those rascals look like, after spending my whole life fighting them? No, Mr Mantis, it was no ant. It was something far more hideous."

"And you did nothing to attract it?"

"I wasn't blowing a bugle, if that's what you mean," snapped the colonel.

The colonel's nephew intervened. "But, Uncle, you *were* whistling in the garden."

"Whistling?" Mantis cocked his head, as if hearing the whistle at that moment.

"Yes, whistling," barked the old warrior. "I suppose I'm not allowed to whistle in my own garden anymore."

"Whistling—*what*, Colonel?" asked Mantis, gently.

"The only thing I ever whistle. The only thing worth whistling. The Pincher's Marching Song."

"A military air . . ."

"Correct," said the colonel, snapping his bootheels together and causing his spurs to jingle.

"Forgive me one more question, Colonel," said Mantis. "Were you wearing those spurred boots, the sound of which we just now heard?"

"I never—" said the colonel coldly, "—wear anything else."

"Thank you, sir," said Mantis. "You've been most helpful."

"Well, I hope you shall be the same." The colonel turned to his nephew. "Show Mantis where the monster went after you."

"Uncle, it will soon be dark . . ."

"I said, show him!" The colonel's monocle flew out on the end of its string, and his nephew snapped to attention.

· · ·

The lantern swung from Springtail's hand, casting eerie shadows on the ground. A fountain played in the darkness ahead of them, with water dripping from a statue, into a little round pool. "I was seated here," said Springtail, pointing to a stone bench. "I had my harmonica out and was playing a tune, very softly . . ."

"More music, Mr Springtail?" Mantis cast a quick glance at the colonel's nephew.

"I play a bit," said Springtail. "Nothing fancy, just a few of the old war songs. I was in the service too, you know . . ."

"And you were playing such a song when the Headless Monster appeared?"

"Yes, Pinchbugs in the Flank. Do you know it?"

"I know it," said Hopper, beginning to hum a few bars.

"That's it," said Springtail, joining in with him.

"Gentlemen, please." Mantis swung about impatiently, snatched the lantern from Springtail, and proceeded to examine the ground for footprints. He moved back and forth near the bench, then off into the grass, returning a moment later with a bitter expression on his face. "Any useful print has been trampled out of all recognition."

"I'm sorry," answered Springtail, "but after our sighting of the monster, all the villagers came to look."

"Regrettable," said Mantis, "but unavoidable, I suppose. We shall have to go into the forest. You haven't been tracking about in there with your villagers, have you?"

"Heavens, no!" Springtail shrank back, curling his tail underneath him. "I wouldn't go in there with less than a regiment."

"I trust that won't be necessary." Mantis lifted the lantern. "Coming along, Doctor?"

Hopper joined Mantis on the narrow path leading into the trees, and a few more steps put them in the dark wood.

"Take care!" called Springtail from the garden, and then his shadowy form sprang away toward the manor.

Mantis moved ahead slowly, searching the ground ahead of him. Hopper remained close at his heels, looking anxiously left and right, seeing headless monsters everywhere. The trees of the great forest danced as the lantern struck them, and the underbrush rustled with scurrying sounds. Mantis bent over, lowering the lantern, then straightened again and moved forward once more, Hopper right beside him. "What do you see, Mantis?" asked Hopper, a high-pitched edge in his voice.

"A great deal, Doctor. And yet—nothing at all."

"Come now, Mantis, don't be obscure. This forest is a most ominous place. If you're on the trail of something, tell me."

Mantis stopped, holding the lantern up, and smiled as the trees swayed and creaked behind him, and the grasses sighed with the night winds. "Do you know the most fearful thing one can ever meet in the darkness, my friend?"

"A Headless Monster?"

"No, Doctor, it is one's own face that is most frightening, should we see it cast as an unfamiliar shadow—" Mantis moved the lantern so that his form became such a shadow, distorted into a monstrous shape, like something seen in a nightmare.

"Are you trying to say that Springtail and everyone else around here have been seeing nothing but their own shadow?"

"The imagination is a powerful force." Mantis lowered the lantern once more, toward the ground. "There is nothing unusual in the footprints I find here. There is nothing—monstrous in them." Again the lantern swung on its handle, and a long spectral shadow danced on the curtain of the forest. "Well, let us return to the manor and wait for sunrise, when this mysterious wood will speak more clearly."

. . .

Hopper lay in his bed, tossing and turning as the last hours of the night passed. A terrible uneasiness had crept over him, and he could not shake it. His regular practice, of counting sheepticks jumping over a fence, hadn't worked. Moreover, he was getting hungry.

He tossed back the other way, and then realized—someone else in the house was as restless as himself: From below in the manor, he heard the sound of a harmonica softly playing.

Springtail is up. Poor chap is a wreck, like myself. Headless Monsters creeping about—and Mantis thinks it's all in our imagination.

Doctor Hopper sank back into his pillow, listening to the old army song that floated up through the air.

*...when I went marching
to the Locust Wars...*

Ah, one of the grand old tunes.

Hopper hummed the melancholy air to himself, bringing back memories of his own days in the service, as an army surgeon far over the sea. Those were dear times that would ne'er return.

*...it's you, Lily-Beetle Marlene
it's you, Lily-Beetle Mar-lene...*

Hopper's head grew heavy, and his leg twitched with sleep. He was sinking down, to the strains of the old tune, into dreamland.

A terrifying shriek from somewhere in the manor house brought him out of bed with a leap. He ran to the door and dashed into the hall, where he met Mantis, and both of them raced down the stairs.

Lamps were being lit through the house, servants hurrying about in their nightshirts, and the center of the confusion was young Springtail, pale, tail trembling, harmonica clutched in his hand as he pointed to the window.

"It was there!" he cried, his voice cracking with terror. "Stalking the grounds!"

"Come, Doctor." Mantis snatched a lantern, and Hopper rushed after him, through the manor door.

The grounds were still covered with fog, only the faintest light of dawn struggling to break through. In a moment, Hopper was separated from Mantis, and found himself groping along through the garden.

The *drip-drip-drip* of the garden pool sounded just ahead of him, and he felt his way toward it slowly. The gravel crunched underneath his feet, and the dripping of the water grew more distinct.

Through the grey mist, he saw the shadowy form of the statue that graced the head of the pool. Water was still dripping from the statue's mouth. He would wait beside it till the sun broke through and the path was clear again. He took two more steps toward it, then added his own terrified shriek to the dawn.

Through the grey mist, he saw the shadowy form of the statue.

"Help! The Monster! Ahhhhhhhhhh . . ."

Hopper stumbled backward, as the statue moved toward him, only it wasn't a statue, it was a hellish nightmare, headless neck dripping, arms reaching toward him.

"Help! Mantis! Springtail! Someone! Help!" Hopper's jumping muscles cocked. In a mere thirtieth of a second, 3500 fibers in each hind leg fired, sending him into a record-breaking high jump, except he tripped on his nightshirt and tumbled backward instead.

"Oh! Oh, no!" He brandished his cane, but the monstrous unseeing thing kept advancing on him, neck drooling, hairy arms waving. The horrible gaping hole that should have been a head was right above him. The hideous arms touched his. He flailed his cane wildly, as a cry stuck in his throat.

Then suddenly a torch came near, and voices broke the fog. The Headless Monster turned, and ran off, vanishing into the morning mist.

"Doctor . . ." Mantis moved in with the lantern.

"The most frightening thing is not one's own face, Mantis," said Hopper, getting up, body shaking. "It is *that*." He pointed toward the bank of fog, through which the creature had gone.

"Very well, Doctor, the monster is real. But what do you make of this?" Mantis lowered the lantern over a heelmark in the mud. "There is the print. It is ordinary. The owner cannot be bigger than—"

"It was gigantic, Mantis!"

"No, Doctor, it was ten millimeters in length."

"But it was *headless*."

The sound of other footsteps on the gravel turned them, toward Springtail, and his uncle, Colonel Bristletail, both of whom were armed. "Mantis, Hopper," growled the Colonel. "Are you all right?"

"We are fine, Colonel," said Mantis.

"My cane," said Hopper. "I dropped it, somewhere back there . . ."

"Here it is, Doctor," said Springtail, reaching into the grass.

"A moment," said Mantis, reaching out his long arm. "What is this liquid upon the tip?"

"From the Monster," said Hopper. "I tried to strike him. He drooled all over it."

"I shall carry your cane, then, Doctor, and be occupied with it for the next hour or so, if you don't mind."

. . .

The ancestral armor room of the manor held swords, shields, and much other weaponry belonging to the old military family. Doctor Hopper walked through it slowly, beneath the flags and banners of the past, when the Bristletail Clan had first conquered the high plateau above the sea. It was all history now, and yet the strangest battle the family had ever fought was in progress at this very hour. Servants went in furtive silence, and every window and door was bolted and watched.

Hopper moved from the armor room, into the hall, and down it to Mantis's room. He knocked gently and entered. The high round shoulders of his friend straightened; Mantis's chemical analysis kit was open on the dresser, where the cane had been carefully placed.

"It is an ordinary saliva solution, Doctor." Mantis pointed at the tip of the cane. "There is no poison, nor any peculiar hormonal secretion. Our monster takes his place within the known families of our race."

"A headless family? Surely not, Mantis."

"He is a fly, Doctor. A large one, I'll grant you, but a fly nonetheless."

"Without a head?"

"Indeed." Mantis removed the jeweler's magnifying glass from his eye and set it down. "Think, Doctor, think back to your army days. Surely you remember decapitation wounds."

"Well, of course, there were such dreadful occurrences—"

"And isn't it so that such a wound, despite its monstrosity, was usually not fatal?" Mantis leaned forward in his chair, pressing his point. "A bug, Doctor, can live without a head."

"Why, we always put the poor devils out of their misery—"

"Just so, Doctor. And you and I are going to put this poor devil out of his misery."

"You mean—"

"He is a Soldier Fly, Doctor. From a battalion that skirmished not far from here, during the Anthill Rebellion of a year ago. Colonel Bristletail will attest to the nearness of that battle, for he was an official observer. There was heavy hand-to-hand fighting, during which, somehow, our monster had his head sliced off. You have been among the ants, Doctor. You know the sort of clean wound they can inflict."

"And he's been wandering ever since—"

"—without a head. He is, moreover, slowly starving to death, for he can't eat. If any part of his mind remains to him, it is undoubtedly suffering the torments of the damned." Mantis stood and stretched his back. "Let us go and collect Colonel Bristletail. He has the bait we need to bring our sad and wretched quarry to its final snare."

. . .

The sun had risen over the high plateau, burning off the mist and illuminating the dancing waves of the ocean that shone far out beyond the manor. Where the cliffside met the forest, a strange little army had formed—Mantis, Hopper, Springtail, and the old colonel, armed with lances from the ancestral armor hall of the Bristletail Clan. Beside them was a uniformed young cicada from the local militia, bearing a military drum.

"Very well," said Mantis, "I think we can begin."

Colonel Bristletail barked a sharp command at the cicada, who started a slow solemn drum roll, which echoed out over the grounds, and over the cliff, to the wide sparkling ocean.

"Forward—*ho!*" The colonel set them marching, and the parade moved along the edge of the forest. Mantis spoke softly to his companions, as their footsteps sounded in rhythm to the drum. "The creature means no harm, I'm certain of that. But he may be maddened beyond control, so should he charge —a swift blow by all. Is that clear?"

"Perfectly," said the colonel. The others nodded, gleaming lances on their shoulders. The drum of the cicada continued to roll, sending its sharp staccato bursts into the air, and Doctor Hopper felt that this must surely be the saddest march that any of them had ever known, despite the military service they'd all endured in the great early wars of Bugland, during which

many lives had been lost. Nonetheless he took a steady grip on his lance, for they were near to the cliff and should the maddened Soldier Fly charge, he could easily knock any of them off the edge of it, into the sea.

"Column right—*march!*"

The colonel barked the command, and the company turned at the edge of the forest, and turned again, coming back. The cicada drum rolled, on and on, tattooing the air with its sound, penetrating the trees, to the very heart of the forest. As the company turned again, a ragged figure moved, just beyond the wall of trees, and all saw it.

The colonel halted the parade, with only the drum continuing, but the forest had become a curtain again, behind which none could know what moved. Hopper brought his lance off his shoulder and prepared to defend.

The drum rolled, and rolled again, and then came the sound of branches breaking underfoot.

Hopper lowered his lance another length, and aimed it at the wall of trees, as beside him Mantis did the same. Colonel Bristletail and his nephew separated from the ranks, forming a second file directly across from Mantis and Hopper, all lances pointing now in a deadly arch, toward the trees.

The crackling in the underbrush came closer. The high grass quivered, then parted, and the headless soldier stepped out, his legs somehow keeping the marching beat of the drum. Slowly, torturously, he marched toward the arch of glittering steel, an arch that suddenly seemed to increase, lance after lance, as if a great company of spirit soldiers were forming to honor this scarred and suffering comrade-at-arms.

The arch of steel glistened brightly, and the headless soldier weaved toward it, his tattered wings hanging, his dragging legs still keeping the beat of the drum. He entered beneath the arch, silently, solemnly, despite the ghastly wound that crowned his form. Headless, sightless, ruined, he marched to the tune of the drum, beneath upraised lances that seemed to extend outward over the ocean to the sun. The eyes of the small living company were moist with tears, even the austere Mantis unable to hold his emotion back; only the company of ghosts were calm, their ghostly swords raised, their ranks ready to receive one who should have joined them long ago in the eternal mist.

The Soldier Fly passed under the steel, toward the cliff, his step seeming to grow stronger as he neared the edge, his form straightening, his monstrous wound forgotten, no longer confusing or demeaning him. He marched, to the drum, over the cliff edge, into the sun.

The ghostly army vanished. The drum ceased. The four living lance-bearers walked quietly to the cliff edge and peered down. The sea, crashing on the rocks far below, had already claimed the headless soldier, whose form would no longer haunt the meadow, nor the forest, nor the field where he had fallen.

THE CASE OF
The Emperor's Crown

"CHECK—AND MATE." Walking Stick moved his knight. Inspector Mantis, seated across from him, stared down at the board in disbelief.

"Sorry, old boy," said Walking Stick, and Doctor Hopper, enjoying the match from an adjacent chair, could not help smiling.

"Another game?" asked Mantis, eager for revenge.

"Oh, let's allow our minds to relax," said Walking Stick, leaning back, deliberately tormenting Mantis a bit.

The waiter came by with more tea, and Doctor Hopper ordered another plate of pollen cakes. At the other tables, the rest of the café regulars were reading newspapers, discussing politics, or meditating in their cups on matters which old, dimly-lit cafés seem to inspire.

"Mantis, Walking Stick, do have one of these little cakes," said Hopper, as the brightly decorated morsels were brought.

"Our friend seems to have lost his appetite," said Walking

Stick, continuing to tease Mantis, who did indeed look morose, long arms folded in his lap, eyes staring toward the café windows.

"I should not have moved the Queen," he said, in a mumble.

"Oh, it goes further back than that," said Walking Stick.

"Now, now, gentlemen, for goodness sake," said Hopper, "let's not replay the entire match. The evening is mild, the crocuses are in bloom, let us think on lighter things. There is more to life than chess, you know."

"Not much more," said Mantis, "for life is a board game."

"So true, so true," said Walking Stick as he munched one of the little cakes. "We stumble along from square to square." He smiled down at the chess board, where Mantis's King still stood in defeat. Mantis caught the glance of triumph and said, "Don't preen yourself too much, Walking Stick, for another game awaits you, as soon as you dare."

"Ah, well," said Walking Stick, "sometimes I tire of check and mate. We should have a different match of wits, some new game."

"If only there were such a one," said Mantis.

"You are the famous detective," said Walking Stick, "who always solves the case. I propose there are three mysteries in Bugland that you cannot solve." The slender bug, tall as Mantis himself, smiled across the table. "Are you for it?"

"Naturally," said Mantis.

"And you, Doctor," said Walking Stick, "will you come along with us and act as judge?"

"I should be happy to."

"I propose there are three mysteries in Bugland that you cannot solve."

At that moment, as the three friends were about to rise,
Police Captain Flatfootfly entered. He looked around, and
then, seeing Mantis, made straight for their table.
"Mantis, I'm glad that I have found you."

"I am honored that you should think
so," said Mantis. "Won't you join us?
We shall order more tea and cakes."

"I haven't time," said Flatfootfly.
But he shuffled his heavy frame into
the fourth chair of the table, and then
turned toward Mantis. "Look here,
I know that sometimes we've gotten
in each other's way, what with one
case and another coming to trouble
our sleep, but I need your help."

"And you shall have it."

"There has been a terrible crime,
one which has not yet been revealed
to the public, for it is a matter of extreme
delicacy—" Captain Flatfootfly looked up,
first at Hopper, then at Walking Stick, and then back to Mantis.

"Please, Captain," said Mantis, "these are my oldest friends.
Walking Stick was with me at school, and Hopper—well, you
know he is the soul of discretion. Whatever case is troubling
you shall not go farther than this table, I assure you."

Flatfootfly stared down, and then said, most quietly, "The
Emperor Moth's crown has been stolen."

The table remained silent for a moment, as all four bugs
contemplated the meaning of the theft—the very symbol of

their country, gone. Mantis finally broke the silence. "Have you any clues?"

"The facts are these," said Flatfootfly. "The crown was scheduled for a grand exhibition tour through all the provinces of Bugland. It was heavily guarded, night and day. But when the grand tour reached its first destination, the province of Anglewing, the crown disappeared."

"I see," said Mantis, his eyes no longer blankly staring at a café window, but seeming to penetrate far into the distance.

"The Emperor's Procession is now returning," said Flatfootfly, "and will soon be nearing the city. I and my men will be there with it—"

"—and I and my friends will be there too, Captain Flatfootfly, be assured of that."

"Thank you, Mantis. I daresay you might be of some little help, might spot some small thing, you know, that we, with our hands full of bigger matters, might miss."

"That is possible." Mantis raised his teacup to his lips, to hide a smile.

"Well, then, I'm off." Flatfootfly huffed to his feet, and puffed away, through the café tables to the door, where his lieutenants awaited him. Walking Stick rose too, with a nod toward Mantis. "I shall leave you to your work, then, Inspector."

"Nonsense," said Mantis. "You must come along. For we have a bet on, you and I, about those three mysteries of Bugland which I'm to solve this night. To the list has been added a fourth, the solution of which might require all our wit put together."

"Very well," said Walking Stick, and the three left their table, where the chess pieces still stood, as if pondering the battle that had so recently been fought.

. . .

A carriage bearing the three friends made its way through the city to meet the Emperor Moth's Procession, and in the distance there had already appeared the first signs of the Emperor's elite military guard—Ambush Bugs marching, to the beat of the drum.

Mantis and his party descended to the side of the road, to join the citizens watching the approach of the parade. The cymbals flashed, the drums thundered, and the Ambushers marched by, a rank of scorpions behind them, stingers raised high, points glistening.

"Ferocious, those lads," said Hopper.

"Certainly are," said Walking Stick. "One wonders how any force could have passed through them, to the crown."

A fierce droning broke the air, followed by a flash of brilliant wings, as the Royal Hornet Squadron flew into view. The yellow-jacketed aviatrixes dove low, ready to attack should it be necessary, and the crowd instinctively drew back.

The way made safe, the Emperor's retinue appeared—a line of Processionary Caterpillars, each of them laying down a silken thread for the Emperor to walk upon.

A murmur swept the crowd, and then the Emperor appeared, striding along over the silken carpet, his glorious wings open, his magnificent robe shining.

"But," said Mantis softly, "no crown."

Doctor Hopper removed his derby and held it over his heart.

"Long Live His Majesty!" shouted the crowd, and Hopper joined the cry. "Long Live His Majesty!"

Doctor Hopper received an elbow in his back, and a coarse voice sounded behind him.

"... comin' through ... beetle with a bottle ..."

It was a Tippling Tommy Beetle, straight from the bottom of a rum barrel. Hiccuping, the drunken lout elbowed past Mantis and Walking Stick, toward the Royal Procession.

"There's a chap," said Hopper, "who might jolly well get a sting he'll never forget."

The Tippling Tommy swayed in the road, then lurched forward, directly toward the Emperor. Two members of the Hornet Squadron swooped down, their arched bodies warning him to go no further, but the tipsy ruffian just bungled forward, singing a song.

"... *oh the Beetle Boys, the Beetle Boys ...*
went out and made ... hiccup ... *a lot of noise ...*"

The two hornets struck, causing the Tippling Tommy to jump, holding the seat of his pants. "... 'ere now ... no need to ... get nasty ..." He stumbled around, heading the other way.

"Remarkable," said Hopper. "They both stung him and he hardly felt it. Must be all the rum he's pickled in."

"*Did* they both sting him?" asked Mantis quietly.

"Why," said Hopper, "you saw it. They both struck at once, a light jab, I'll admit, but two shots from a hornet's tail—"

Mantis motioned Hopper with him, toward the bumbling beetle, who'd just dropped his flask, and was in the process of bending over to get it, the vulgar song once again on his lips.

"... *oh the Beetle Boys, the Beetle Boys*

were never much ... hiccup ... *for social poise* ..."

Mantis pointed. "The seat of his pants, Doctor, aside from being covered with burrs, dandelion fluff, and mud, bears the mark of the hornets' attack. You'll note there is but one puncture in the cloth ..."

"So there is. But what does *that* mean?"

"I do not know, Doctor. But it is, as our friend Flatfootfly has said, one of the 'little things.'"

Mantis turned back toward the procession, which Captain Flatfootfly and his men had now joined, marching beside the Ambush Bugs. Flatfootfly saw Mantis, and gave a nod, which Mantis returned, as the parade went by.

"I think we've learned all we can from this vantage point, Doctor. Let us collect Walking Stick and move on." Mantis looked around for his tall friend. "But where has he gotten to?"

"There he is," said Hopper, pointing into the roadside park, toward a little lake, where Walking Stick stood, gazing out over the water.

"A dreamy sort of fellow," said Mantis, striding with Hopper into the park to fetch Walking Stick. "I'll never know how such a mind could possibly be skillful at chess, but the fact remains—"

"—he frequently defeats you."

"It must be some sort of blind chance, that's all I can make of it."

"Now, Mantis, don't be snide."

Mantis strode ahead, calling toward the water. "Come, Walking Stick. We've no time for idling."

The towering bug turned. "Idling? We have a wager, my friend. Or have you forgotten already?"

Mantis blinked dully for a moment, then joined Walking Stick at the edge of the water, where a party of Whirligig Beetles were skimming along, circling, turning, their little bodies shining like black pearls.

"Well?" asked Mantis, looking at them, and then at Walking Stick.

"A moment, Mantis, a moment more. Look upon them, please." Walking Stick returned his gaze to the Whirligigs, as did Mantis. The bright creatures were moving here, there, and everywhere with great determination, twirling, whirling, looping and spinning, their fevered movement cutting momentary patterns in the water, which shivered, and died away.

"A senseless occupation," said Mantis. "They are frivolous types."

"Indeed?" Walking Stick continued to gaze at them with rapt attention. "Then you have already lost the first of my three challenges."

"Lost it?" exclaimed Mantis. "I haven't even heard it."

"You've seen it," said Walking Stick, pointing at the rippling lines the Whirligigs made on the water. "There is the first great mystery of Bugland."

"I fail to see—"

"Quite so, you fail to see, what none but they can see." Walking Stick gestured out over the edge of the pond with his slender arm, as the Whirligigs whirled past. "They write upon the water, Mantis, words that vanish forever, only to be written again a moment later. Over and over they write, the story of the Whirligig. Read it to me, my friend. Read what is written on the water . . ." Walking Stick smiled, as Mantis stared dumbly at the display. The Whirligigs whirled, and Mantis saw for an instant, a letter, then another, and another, written so swiftly and gone so quickly that he could make no sense out of it at all. But that sense was there he could not doubt, for the whole pond, he saw now, was like a blackboard made of glass, over which the Whirligigs raced, shaping their mysterious story. He reached out his arm, as if to touch it, then let his arm drop, knowing he was beaten.

"Well," said Walking Stick, still smiling, "I don't mean to keep you from your official duties." He bowed toward their waiting carriage. "If you wish to now pursue the culprit who carted off the crown—"

"Yes," muttered Mantis, "yes, let's do that," and Doctor Hopper noticed the detective's form had fallen into a despondent slouch, Walking Stick's first mystery of Bugland weighing heavily on his shoulders. It has not, thought Doctor Hopper, been a good afternoon for him. First Walking Stick beats him at chess, and now this . . .

Walking Stick clapped Mantis on the back. "Cheer up, old fellow. You have the missing crown ahead of you. You'll find it, surely."

"Crown, yes," mumbled Mantis. As they stepped up to the carriage, he glanced at Walking Stick, and shook his head, as if Walking Stick had played a despicable trick on him.

"He's not a good loser," said Hopper softly, to Walking Stick.

• • •

Once again, it was the Duchess of Doodlebug who arranged for them to enter the court as if they were private guests rather than a team of investigators. "I'm so happy to be showing you around His Majesty's grounds, Doctor. Aren't they delightful?"

"Yes, Duchess, they are most inspiring," said Hopper, walking with the Duchess, while Mantis and Walking Stick poked around in other of the royal niches, each of them watching for a word, a glance, a suspicious movement from some member of the royal household who might have been part of the crime.

"The plant life in the garden is so thrilling—" The Duchess gestured at the many exotic flowers hanging over them, attended by gardener bugs of every variety. Hopper sized them all up—the palace moths with long proboscises which they inserted tenderly into the flowers, followed by worker bees with their pollen cups. None of them looked the slightest bit suspicious—they were devoted servants of the court.

"Tell me, Doctor—" The Duchess leaned in toward Hopper, her voice falling to a whisper. "—what is your real purpose in being here? Now, don't try to deceive me. I know that you are investigating something with those two friends of yours. Has something happened to His Majesty? He has been looking quite distressed."

"Duchess, please, I'm not at liberty—"

"Oh, I love a mystery so! Do confide in me, Doctor."

"Duchess, I should like nothing better, for I loathe a mystery. Let life be out in the open, I say, let the sun shine, let—"

"Doctor—" The Duchess tapped the toe of her shoe on the stone path. "—you're evading my question."

"Duchess, you must forgive me, I—"

"I shan't forgive you," said the Duchess, withdrawing her arm from his. "And you may just walk by yourself in the garden." She glided off, leaving Hopper to stroke his mustache in confusion.

A powerful droning overhead announced the Royal Hornet Squadron, circling the palace, ever vigilant against intruders. Hopper watched the fierce female fliers zoom in over the garden, the sunlight in their wings and dangerous dedication in their searching eyes. Ridiculous, thought Hopper, for Mantis to see anything suspect about that branch of the service. Those courageous creatures are as loyal as he is, and beautiful, to boot.

The colorful band of aviatrixes climbed high again over the flowers, their bright uniforms streaked as if by the sun itself, and Hopper walked along, head back, admiring the curves of their flight. Splendid, simply splendid, I wonder if I might possibly ask one of them to lunch with me.

"Uff—" A collision on the path sent him stumbling backward. "Forgive me, I wasn't watching . . ."

"No, you wasn't." An angry bee stood before him, hair ruffled, wings whirring in place. "Be more careful next time, or—"

"Yes, certainly, my fault, absolutely . . ." Hopper walked quickly on, rather shocked at the rough attitude of the bee. Workers at the Royal Court are supposed to be refined, or at least they once were. Well, things have changed, I suppose . . .

Suddenly, beside him, the bushes moved. Made cautious by his recent collision, he jumped out of the way, but then saw a familiar face.

"Flatfootfly!"

"*Sssssshhhhhhh . . .*" Flatfootfly peered out suspiciously. "Have you seen anything?"

"Well," said Hopper, "the bees at work in this garden are rather rude. Not at all what one would expect."

"*That,*" said Flatfootfly, "is a useless observation. Have you nothing more to report?"

"No," said Hopper, "not a thing."

The bushes closed around Flatfootfly, and Hopper watched the policeman's bulky form pushing its way along through the foliage, toward the other end of the path, where Walking Stick had just appeared. Flatfootfly peered out at Walking Stick, then disappeared once more, rustling onward.

Walking Stick joined Hopper on the path. "I've had the official tour—the Throne Room, the Tower, the Flowering Wall— but as for suspicious characters, there's the only one I've encountered." Walking Stick pointed toward the bulging bushes, where Flatfootfly was prowling.

"And where is Mantis?"

"He said that we should meet him in the barracks of the Bombardier Beetles. I believe it's this way." They left the garden and circled the outer grounds, to the rear of the palace, where, on an enormous open field, a platoon of Bombardier Beetles was practicing maneuvers. Powerful detonations were going off from the Bombardiers' abdomens, and the field was filled with floating gas.

"I served next to the Bombardiers in the Locust Wars," said Hopper, as he and Walking Stick crossed at the edge of the field. "That gas of theirs will flatten a toad."

A Bombardier Guard stepped in front of them. "Passes, please."

Hopper handed over his pass. "We're looking for a friend—"

"Tall fellow? Likes to play cards?"

"Cards?" Hopper cringed. "Is he gambling again?"

The guard pointed toward a long white barracks. "In there, playing with some of our crowd. A reckless sort of bidder, I might add. He was losing his shirt, last I looked in on the game."

"Thank you," said Hopper. "Come, Walking Stick, let's gather him up before he loses next month's rent, as well as this."

They walked quickly to the barracks door and entered. Within, a group of Bombardiers were seated around a table, drinking ambrosia, with smoke curling over their heads and cards in their hands. Mantis sat among them, pipe smoldering, his brow creased in a frown. Upon the table in front of him was a considerable wager in money, topped off by his pocket watch, and he was now calling for another card. The Bombardier dealer snapped it to him, Mantis took it, sighed, and laid down a losing hand. His money and watch were taken by a smiling Bombardier, and Mantis turned away, head hanging low, but when he saw Hopper and Walking Stick his manner brightened.

"Ah, my friends, just in time—" He indicated the shuffling cards, which were being prepared for the next hand.

"I shan't lend you money, Mantis," said Hopper.

"No, I suppose not. Well, then—" Mantis pushed away from the table and the Bombardiers gave him a jovial salute, as they counted his money and examined his watch. "Come back again, sir," said the dealer. "Always welcome . . ."

"Yes, I daresay." Mantis walked to the door, where an officer of the Bombardiers was holding his cape for him.

"You'll have better luck next time, Inspector."

"Thank you, Major, I'm sure I shall." Mantis straightened himself into his cape and walked with calm dignity through the doorway, Hopper and Walking Stick following him.

"Mantis," said Hopper, "will you never learn?"

"Had I drawn the ace—"

"A child could beat him at cards," said Hopper to Walking Stick as they walked on through the camp yard. "At least, Mantis, I hope you learned something."

"I learned," said Mantis, "how the Bombardier Beetles fire their explosive charge. They carry two hydroquinone compounds in their weapons glands. When the mixture is ignited in an internal reaction chamber, the blast is—"

"—the crown, Mantis. What about the crown?"

Mantis stopped on the path and relit his pipe. "One month ago, an imposter wearing the uniform of the Bombardiers was discovered. He was arrested, and put under military guard, but he managed to escape, apparently with help from inside the palace." Mantis threw his match away. "Aside from losing my pocket watch, that was the only unexpected turn of events the day has brought me. Did either of you uncover anything of interest?"

"I uncovered Captain Flatfootfly," said Walking Stick. "Or rather, he popped out at me from the bushes."

"Yes," said Mantis, "everyone in the palace has noted his attempts at hiding himself. He should appear right about—*there*—I think, in a moment or two." Mantis pointed toward the shrubs that lined the shaded side of the palace, and as he and Hopper and Walking Stick approached them, the shrubbery bulged outward, and a pair of large flat feet appeared down around the roots.

"Captain Flatfootfly," said Mantis, "good afternoon."

"*Sssssshhhhhhhhhhh,*" said a voice from the shrubbery, and the flat feet flapped back, out of sight.

"Flatfootfly is handling the bigger matters, as he calls them, with his usual delicacy. Leaving the small ones entirely to us. What of your observations in the garden, Doctor? Anything out of the ordinary there?"

"No," said Hopper, "only a very rude bee. His Majesty's staff is not what it once was, when it comes to good manners."

"Let us just duck into the garden," said Mantis, "and have a look at this ill-mannered bee of yours."

"We need go no further," said Hopper, pointing with his cane toward the gates of the garden. "There's the specimen, directly ahead."

The bee was moving past the gates, with another bee, both in subdued conversation. Mantis blinked once, gazing at them with marked interest. Then, without comment, he turned away, appearing to be studying the petals of a rose as the bees passed by. "Well," he said, when the bees had disappeared, "we must leave the palace now, and do a little digging."

"Did you see something?" asked Hopper. "In those bees?"

"Oh, not much," said Mantis, as they headed toward the outer wall of the palace. "Indeed, only one small detail. Another 'little thing,' if you will."

"And what is that?" asked Walking Stick.

"Bees have two sets of wings," said Mantis. "Those creatures had only one." The inspector tapped his pipe ash out into his palm and scattered it in the wind. "A wasp without a sting— and a bee without a wing. Most interesting. Most interesting, indeed."

· · ·

The great library held long tables, at which scholars of all kinds sat, bent over large tomes. In their midst, Mantis had made a place, and was working through a formidable volume on insect camouflage. The librarian had already scolded him three times for lighting his pipe. Reduced, therefore, to chewing nervously on it, he'd bitten clean through the mouthpiece. But now he suddenly straightened, took the pipe from his mouth and traced a line with the ruined pipestem across the page before him.

"That's it! Exactly as I thought!"

"*Sssssshhhhhhhhhhhh* . . ." Scholars on both sides admonished him, but Walking Stick came quickly over, to join him in his find.

"What is it?"

Mantis pointed to the page, and the line. "Do you see?"

Walking Stick read closely, nodding his head. "Yes, yes, certainly. Clear as day . . ."

"*Will* you be quiet?" snapped an elderly bookworm.

"Forgive us," said Mantis, slamming his volume closed with an excited *bang* which shook the other scholars in their seats, and caused dark mutterings to break from their close-sealed lips.

". . . unspeakable nuisance . . ."

". . . has broken *every* rule of silence . . ."

". . . have the librarian pitch him out . . ."

Walking Stick steered Mantis toward his own table. "Here's all I could find on silk. Is this what you wanted?"

Mantis glanced down, reading quickly. "Excellent, Walking

Stick! We are closing fast!" Mantis moved quickly to the end of the table where Doctor Hopper was seated, engrossed in a study of the Sunday funny papers, several issues of which he'd missed, owing to chasing around Bugland with Mantis.

"Come, Doctor—" Mantis took the little chap by one elbow, and Walking Stick grabbed the other. Together the two towering bugs lifted the doctor from his chair.

"I say!" shouted Hopper. "Just a moment! I must learn what happened to Wonder Worm!"

The librarian pounced on them. "*Out!*" she ordered in a commanding whisper. "*At once!*"

Hopper removed his derby, attempting to apologize, while Walking Stick tried to explain that Mantis was a well-known detective at work on a case. The librarian shoved them out the door and locked it behind her.

"A firm disciplinarian," said Mantis.

"Well, if you hadn't yanked me out of my seat—" Hopper picked his derby off the steps, where it had landed in the shuffle.

"Dear friends," said Walking Stick, "before we rush back to the palace, may we—?" He gestured toward a ruined old factory nearby, its windows out, its doors hanging off. "There's something in that place that we might have a look at."

"There's not time," said Mantis. "We must—" Then he stopped, looked at Walking Stick, his brow furrowed again. "Our wager? About the three mysteries of Bugland?"

"This is the second of them," said Walking Stick, with a smile.

"Very well," said Mantis glumly, and followed Walking Stick along the street, into the ruined building.

"It was a mill," said Walking Stick, as they walked in the echoing gloom of the place. "It's nothing but a derelict now, slowly being eaten away."

Mantis and Hopper looked upward, to where Walking Stick pointed. On the wooden rafters an elderly Engraver Beetle was at work, chewing his way along through the wood.

"Tell me, Inspector," said Walking Stick, "what has the Engraver written? What is the meaning of his hieroglyph?"

Mantis stared at the peculiar squiggle of lines the old Engraver had left behind him. "Why it—has no meaning. It's just aimless wandering."

Walking Stick bent his head back, calling upward. "Hallo, there!"

"Eh?" The elderly Engraver turned on his rafter, and looked down.

Walking Stick pointed at Mantis and Hopper. "We're from the newspaper. We'd like to know what your patterns mean."

The Engraver paused, staring down at them in silence for a moment. Then he looked back along the way he'd come, over the strange winding arabesque he'd carved in the wood, and his gaze was like that of one in a trance, and his crackly old voice echoed in the shadowy dome. *It's the story—of me life.*

He lowered his head, and went back to work, chewing his way forward.

Walking Stick looked at Mantis, but the inspector had already turned, toward the door.

. . .

"Duchess, if you would accept please, this small offering . . ." Hopper handed the grand old beauty a bouquet, as Mantis and Walking Stick bowed with him, all three attending to the very important matter of getting on the Duchess's good side again.

She sniffed the bouquet and gave them a tentative smile of forgiveness. "Does this mean," she said coyly, "you're going to tell me what all your mysterious doings are about?"

Mantis stepped forward. "I'm afraid, Duchess, our explanation will only add mystery to mystery. His Majesty has suffered a grievous loss of property. To regain it for him, we must be able to attend the Hornet Squadron's banquet tonight in the palace. Moreover, we need to make a switch in the napkins."

"In the *nap*-kins?"

"The napkins in use at the Hornet's Hall are made of paper. Tonight they shall be replaced with silk." Again Mantis bowed over the grande dame's hand. "Will you cast your lot with us, dear lady? And help to regain—the crown?"

The eyes of Duchess Doodlebug opened wide, and the gathered flowers slipped from her arms. *"The crown?"* she whispered in disbelief.

"Silk," said Mantis softly. "From your own dining table. Enough for the entire Hornet Squadron."

"You shall have it," said the Duchess.

. . .

Hopper entered the banquet room in black tie and tails, bearing a large silver tray. "M'lady," he said, serving the Commander of the Hornets. At the other end of the table, Mantis and Walking Stick, also in the guise of butlers, were serving the rest of the Squadron. The beautiful aviatrixes clicked their glasses together, toasting their commander, and conversation began around the table, as Mantis, Walking Stick, and Hopper circled—bringing more ambrosia, more rose petals, more beebread.

The eyes of the hornet fliers were sparkling, their yellow and black dress uniforms splendid their buzzing laughter covering the metallic glint of natures proud, deadly, and loyal to the court. Ambrosia flowed, the buzz of conversation grew brighter, and course followed course. Napkins were flourished, the aviatrixes daintily wiping their hands, touching at their lips, until—

"*There*," hissed Mantis to Walking Stick, and both of them saw—on the napkin of one of the fliers, a sudden stain of brown had appeared. The stain spread, the napkin began to disintegrate, and the aviatrix looked about her in confusion, then threw the napkin quickly down.

'That is she," said Mantis, through the kitchen doorway, to Flatfootfly, who, wearing a high chef's hat and a white apron, moved into the room. "I arrest you," he said, "for the theft of the crown."

The suspect leapt up, knocking her chair backward. "Don't come near me!" Her body arched into the stinging position.

"She'll not fire on you, Captain Flatfootfly," said Mantis quietly. "For she has no sting. She is in fact no hornet at all, but only—a moth."

An angry shock swept the table of fliers, and only the intervention of Flatfootfly and Mantis saved the helpless moth from instant death.

"I didn't mean to be part of it," she sobbed, her stern military bearing falling away. "They made me do it."

"Who made you do it?" asked Flatfootfly.

"The Robber Flies! They sought me out to help them steal the crown, because my camouflage is that of the hornet." The moth gestured with her wings, which so perfectly matched those of the squadron. "They took the crown, they have it hidden."

"And where," asked Flatfootfly, "might those Robber Flies be?"

"In the garden," said Mantis, "in their own natural camouflage—that of the bee. Is that not right, my dear?"

"Yes," sobbed the moth. "They worked their way into the staff, one by one—"

"You mean," exclaimed Flatfootfly, "them bees in the garden aren't really—bees?"

"When you arrest them," said Mantis, "take note of their wings. One set instead of two. A 'little' thing, Captain which—"

Flatfootfly shouted to his lieutenants. "Round up the Robber Flies! One set of wings instead of two!"

The Commander of the Hornets stepped forward, her fierce eyes glowing. "We shall round them up."

Brilliant sabers flashed, and a terrible whirring filled the room as the Hornet Squadron rushed to the door.

Doctor Hopper set his butler's tray down on the empty table, and took a chair, before a large dessert plate. "No need to let this aphid ice cream go uneaten, is there? No, I think not." And he dipped his spoon into the delicious sweet.

. . .

"But how did you know," asked the Duchess of Doodlebug, "that the imposter was a moth, and that her napkin would turn brown?"

Mantis paused at the palace gates, Hopper and Walking Stick by his side. "There are several insects who impersonate the hornet, but the most convincing is the moth, who can deceive any bird, any toad, with her performance. However, silk is her one betrayer . . ."

"But what is so special about silk?"

"When exiting its silken cocoon," said Mantis, "the moth produces a powerful saliva which softens the silk and allows the moth to escape. In the process, the silk is stained brown. Therefore, we had to make the entire Hornet Squadron use silk, and then wait for the stain to appear, which it did, from the lips of the moth."

"Oh, that *is* remarkable! How did you ever learn such a thing?"

"It cost me my library card," interrupted Hopper bitterly.

"And now I'll have to buy the Sunday funny papers, instead of reading them for free."

"I'm sure you'll be forgiven, Doctor," said the Duchess.

"*I'm* not," said Hopper. "Mantis made a scandalous racket."

The guard at the palace gates clicked his heels. "We are closing the grounds to all visitors now."

"Yes, we're about to run along," said Mantis. "Goodbye, Duchess. It has been a pleasure, as always."

"The Crown of Bugland has been returned," said the Duchess, pointing to the blazing lights of the palace. "It shall not stray again."

"I should hope not," said Mantis. "Once is quite enough."

The large gates swung slowly closed, and the three bugs walked out onto ordinary ground again, beneath a glowing city streetlamp.

"Perhaps," said Mantis, turning to Walking Stick, "we might find an open chess table at our café."

"Righto," said Walking Stick. "But before we leave the vicinity, I noticed something a little earlier this evening which I'd like to bring to your attention. It's just over this way, in the bushes . . ."

"Not Flatfootfly again, I hope?" asked Mantis.

"No," said Walking Stick, drawing the bushes aside. "It is something that hides itself more quietly than Flatfootfly."

Mantis and Hopper looked into the shadows, at a thing most solemn, most silent, most still. Common as the sight might be, the three bugs gazed at it in fascination, for of all things found in the world, there is nothing to compare to the sculpted beauty of the insect pupa.

"I arrest you," he said, *"for the theft of the crown."*

The pupa hung before them, awesome in its silent vigil, the sacred cowl wrapped around its head, arms folded on its chest, half-hidden eyes seeming to contemplate eternity through a mummy's mask.

"Tell me—of what does the sleeping pupa dream?" Walking Stick glanced up from the mummy. "For that, my friend, is the third, and greatest, mystery of Bugland."

Mantis spoke softly, into the shadows. "We—cannot know."

Walking Stick let the bushes close up again, and laid his hand gently on his companion's shoulder. "Come along. It is indeed time for us to see about a table at our café." He turned to Hopper. "Are you with us, Doctor?"

"Oh, yes, quite," said Hopper, and the three friends made their way along the winding street, leaving the sleeping pupa to its deep and secret dream.